MEDIA can do wonders in students' life

S.S. Dogra

MEDIA
can do wonders in students' life

S.S. Dogra

pblishing.com
write • share • connect • publish

Media can do wonders in students' life
by Surender Singh Dogra

Published by www.pblishing.com

pblishing.com
write • share • connect • publish

Marketed by

Maple Press Private Limited
sales office A 63, Sector 58, Noida 201 301, U.P., India
phone +91 120 455 3581, 455 3583
email info@maplepress.co.in
website www.maplepress.co.in

ISBN: 978-81-93324-83-7

Printed in India

10 9 8 7 6 5 4 3 2 1

Dedicated to...

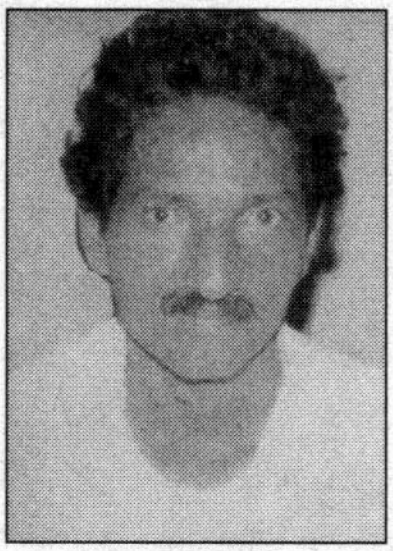

Lt. Thakur Partap Singh Ji

My father has been a great source of inspiration for me since my childhood. His thoughts & vision towards education are still very much within me.

Lt. Joginder Singh Ji

I am also great fan & follower of **Late Joginder Singh ji (Retd. IPS & former Director C.B.I.)**. I learnt many things from him like honesty, simplicity, sincerity & love for writing during our bonding of more than two decades.

I dedicate this book to both noble souls whose.
Blessings are the real strength for me.

अरविंद कुमार सिंह (वरिष्ठ पत्रकार)
प्रमुख, संसदीय कार्यक्रम विभाग,
राज्य सभा टीवी, भारतीय संसद
12 ए, गुरुद्वारा रकाबगंज,
नयी दिल्ली 110001

प्रस्तावना

तमाम उतार चढ़ाव के बाद भी स्वतंत्रता आंदोलन से लेकर आज तक पत्रकारिता का महत्व बढ़ता जा रहा है। आज इसका स्वरूप बहुआयामी हो गया है। संचार क्रांति ने इसे बहुत विस्तार दे दिया है और इस कारण पत्रकारिता के क्षेत्र में चुनौतियां बढ़ी हैं। एक तरह से कहें तो आज विशेषज्ञता का युग आ गया है। तमाम क्षेत्रों में जो भी बेहतर प्रदर्शन करेगा वह आगे बढ़ेगा और इस कारण भारी होड़ के बाद भी गुणवत्ता की मांग बनी रहेगी। शायद इसी कारण हाल के सालों में पत्रकारिता शिक्षा का काफी विस्तार हुआ है और बड़ी संख्या में छात्र पत्रकारिता पाठ्यक्रमों में दाखिला ले रहे हैं। लेकिन उनको स्तरीय पाठय पुस्तकों की कमी से जूझना पड़ता है। पत्रकारिता के इतिहास और तमाम पक्षों पर वैसे तो किताबों की कमी नहीं हैं। लेकिन उसके लेखकों में अधिकतर वे लोग हैं जिनका पत्रकारिता से सीधा सरोकार नहीं रहा है । इस नाते जब छात्र कैंपस से निकलने के बाद सच्चाई के धरातल पर पहुंचते हैं तो उनको यह शिक्षा खास काम नहीं आती है। स्कूली बच्चों को पत्रकारिता के बाह्य स्वरूप के बारे में ही जानकारी होती है। उनके पास इस विषय की समझ के लायक पुस्तक नहीं है।

वरिष्ठ पत्रकार और मेरे अभिन्न सहयोगी श्री एस. एस. डोगरा ने अपनी पुस्तक “Media Can do wonders in Students' Life” में इस कमी को दूर करने का प्रयास किया है। श्री डोगरा पत्रकारिता में बहुआयामी व्यक्तित्व के धनी हैं और दो दशकों की पत्रकारिता में उन्होंने कृषि से लेकर खेलों, बॉलीवुड, पर्यटन, राजनीतिक क्षेत्र के लेखन में खास प्रतिष्ठा अर्जित की है। और बेहतरीन फोटो पत्रकार की प्रतिभा को भी निखारा है।

मेरे नेतृत्व में दिल्ली पत्रकार संघ में भी श्री डोगरा ने सराहनीय योगदान दिया था। पत्रकारिता के तमाम पक्षों की जमीनी हकीकत से वे अच्छी तरह परिचित रहे हैं और उनका निजी अनुभव व्यापक है। इस पुस्तक के तमाम सोपानों से उन्होंने मेरे और तमाम वरिष्ठ पत्रकार मित्रों से समय समय पर सलाह ली है। इस नाते मुझे लगता है कि यह बहुत उपयोगी पुस्तक होगी।

श्री डोगरा द्वारा लिखित पुस्तक “Media Can do wonders in Students' Life” अंग्रेजी में है लेकिन यह हिंदी और भारतीय भाषाओं के पत्रकारिता के छात्रों के लिए समान रुप से उपयोगी है। मैं कामना करता हूं कि इसका अन्य भाषाओं में अनुवाद होगा और पत्रकारिता के शिक्षक इसे महत्व देंगें।

Dr. Ashok Lav
(Educationist, Journalist & Poet)
President-International Hindi Association,
America (Delhi & NCR Chapter)
Flat-363, Surya Apartments, Sector-6,
Dwarka, New Delhi-110 075

Foreword

Media is a channel or medium by which people communicate through internet, television, newspapers, magazines, radio and films. Internet has changed the life style of people by using social network like Facebook, Micro-blogging like Twitter, weblog, social blog, Instagram etc. These are computers mediated technologies by which people create and share expressions, information, ideas and interests. They posts texts, videos, digital photographs.

People across the world are connected with each other through internet. This made the world a global village. The electronic media has disseminated the knowledge and information internationally. This has changed the world of education also. Modern students are more dependent on e-media. They get latest information through internet related virtual communities like facebook, YouTube and many apps.

My friend Mr. S.S. Dogra in his book "Media Can Do Wonders in Students' Life" has covered all aspects of e-media and print-media. He is directly involved in educating students & inspiring them to use the media in positive manners. So far he has conducted many Media Workshop & two mega Media Conclaves for school and college students in many parts of India.

This book is very useful for students because Mr. Dogra shared his academic & practical experience in the book. He himself is a sincere media person, a senior Journalist and Post Graduate in Journalism and Mass Communication.

'Mass Media Studies and Production' are the parts of C.B.S.E. syllabus now. Therefore, this book is very useful as a reference book also. The school going students who want to make their career in Journalism must read this book because it covers topics ranging from understanding media, communications, e-media, print-media and Journalism etc.

This book provides a valuable window on media.

I am honored to know Mr. S.S. Dogra, a dedicated and vibrant media personality.

Sh. Nabin Jha
Additional Director, Secretariat Lok Sabha,
Govt. of India, New Delhi-110001

Message

Can we imagine a family without any means of communications? No, Absolutely No. Similarly, if today's world is an extended family (KUTUMB), it is simply because of MEDIA, a prominent and a powerful means of communication, to know he News & Views of people around the globe. No doubt, media can do wonders in everybody's life including the students' life also. Students are the future of any nation. Fully informed students are the strength of a nation. Media can shape or reshape the future of this world through the students.

There are so many books on media describing their roles, duties, responsibilities and sermonizing them. But they are of little significance for the school going children. Recognizing this very need of the students. Sh. S.S.Dogra has taken a very good initiative through his book "Media can do wonders in students' Life" probably the first ever in this direction. Particularly, the Unit II,III & IV of this are very useful for the school going students. Names, addresses of Media Universities/colleges/institutes in India are also very helpful for those interested in Mass Communication. The students can learn many things about writing skills also. The living examples and practical experience showed by Dogra ji who himself a sincere media person & Post Graduate in Journalism & Mass Communication. His book "Media can do wonders in students' Life" is a worth reading.

I am honored to be associated with him for the last more than ten years. A hearty congratulation to him for this book on Media.

I hope that this book will prove to be a milestone for the students right from class VI to XII and also for those interested in making their career in the field of Media.

With Regards.
Nabin Jha

Sandeep Marwah
Founder Director of Asian
Academy of Film & Television
Director-Asian School of Media Studies.
Founder of Film City, Noida,

Dear Mr. Dogra,
I went through the book "Media can do wonders in students' life" and I am sure it will be of immense use to the youngsters of today. The way role of media has been explained, it could have been done only by a seasoned media person that you are.
I wish you all the success for the book.
Best regards

Dr. Ashok Ogra
Director, Apeejay Institute of
Mass Communication, New Delhi
Formerly : Vice President, Discovery Channel &
Animal Planet (South Asia)
www.apeejay.edu/aimc
www.facebook.com/apjmasscomm

Today, when two out of the five pillars of Indian democracy i.e. media & the social media have democratized information, media has become an integral source of information. It facilitates building and shaping public opinion, and persuading citizens into action. It also helps promoting political ideologies - the bedrock of a democratic polity.

A course in mass communication from a reputed institute/college helps aspiring students to learn the 'How to' aspect of journalism with a critical 'Why' perspective so important in an environment that is dynamic and ever changing.

A formal and well structured training helps students in information gathering, data interpretation and finally reporting in a manner that is unbiased and truthful, and provides all shades of public opinion.

Yours is an excellent endeavour in this regard.

अनिल पाण्डेय
(अध्यक्ष-दिल्ली पत्रकार संघ)

वर्तमान समय में मीडिया की एक नकारात्मक तस्वीर पेश की जा रही है। एस. एस. डोगरा जी ने अपनी पुस्तक मीडिया कैन डू वंडर्स इन स्टूडेंट्स लाइफ" के माध्यम से इसकी एक सकारात्मक तस्वीर पेश की है और छात्रों को बताया है कि थोड़ा समय टीवी और अखबार के साथ बिताने से कैसे उनका भविष्य संवर सकता है। यह छात्रों के लिए उपयोगी पुस्तक साबित होगी।

Tinna Ghaai
Bollywood Actor & Singer
(Mumbai, MH)

Media has a very important role in our life. Interestingly, there are two types of media persons one who works negatively and other positively.

I know Mr. S.S. Dogra for the past five years and found him very honest, sincere , transparent. He is Media person who is actively involved in this thankless profession. I am sure his latest book "Media can do wonders in Students' life" will really do wonders in their life too. My best wishes are always with him.

My Expression...

Education and media can together bring prosperity in the human life and even the entire universe. Yes, this is a fact. Here I am sharing an interesting story: my father & mother were totally illiterate and they even could not write the Hindi alphabets. I learnt the English alphabets in VI class but recently my daughter Sakshi who after completing her B. Tech. (Computer Science) just joined an MNC as an Associate Computer Engineer. This is an instant example and proud moment for our family and for everyone concerned. The Education, moral values, patience, honesty, sincerity, dedication, transparency, commitment with proper utility of media always brings positive results in life, so, it is our duty to work accordingly and make our life more meaningful.

Let me share an important thing that how I got the idea to write a book that too on media. As you know that I always love to interact with the students. Luckily, two years ago, Mrs. Nita Arora, Principal of Sri Venkateshwar International School, gave me the opportunity to conduct a media workshop with IX class students. That was the foundation and after that I conducted several Media workshops in Delhi and NCR but again Mrs. Jaspreet Kaur-Vice Principal of Bal Bhavan International School and students of her school impressed. Mr. Kunal Gupta-Principal of Bal Bhavan International School offered me to join the school as P.G.T. (Media Studies) Visiting Faculty. Here I was given XII class to teach. After a few classes a student, Piyush pointed out that the books on media studies are not available in the market so I seriously thought over it. Meantime, Kunal Gupta sir empowered me to organize a Media Literacy Conclave on 3rd Dec., 2016 in Bal Bhavan Intl. school where a book "Eminent World Scientists" (authored by Cicily Kodiyan aunty and edited by me) was released. That was the turning point and I started exploring to write my own book on Media and rest is history in your hand.

But to find a good publisher is a big issue, fortunately, I went to Mr. Prince Kohli (reputed Book Distributer) whom I expressed my desire to print a book, he guided me to meet Rajitha Madam-Maple Publishers and ultimately my dreams come true.

I acknowledge my mother Sneh Lata ji who always motivate me even in the adversity, My role model in the Journalism field Sh. Arvind Kumar Singh ji, Sh.Manohar Singh ji, all my relatives, friends, well wishers, all my colleague & my students, Sanjay Mishra Sir who always stands with me, Sandeep Marwah Sir who always encourages me, MCPS family-Sh. M. S. Yadav Sir, Sudha Data Madam, Neeru Madam, Sarita Madam, Dwivedi Sir, Manisha Mam, Mohsin ji, Writer Sushil Bharti ji, Ms. Neha Kala-Social Activist, Dr. Amit Kaur-Scientist & Author, Mrs. Anuradha Govind-Principal-J. M. International School, Mrs. Rashmi Malik-Delhi International School, Mrs. Manju Tiwari-Principal, CRPF School, Dr. Mrinalini Kaur-Director and Mrs. Manisha Sharma-Principal -Venkateshwar Intl. School, Dr. Raji Kumar-Principal, N. K. Bagrodia School, Mrs. Anju Mahrotra-Principal, Kalka Public School whose encouragement gave me the confidence to move ahead. Last but not the least Dr. K. Y. Benedict- Principal, Mar Theophilus Training College, who invited me as a resource person (Sponsored by UGC) and authorized me to conduct the 2nd Media conclave parallel to their International Seminar held in their Nalanchira, Trivananthapuram, Kerala campus from 1-3 March, 2017. The poster of my book was launched here itself. The encouragement from scholar Dr. Ashok Lav sir who himself an exemplary literary personality for me and Prof. (Dr.) Prasannanshu's final touch made my writing efforts more significant. My wife Sunita and daughter always helped me in this mission. The passion of my dearest students Utkarsh, Shubham, Satyam, Honey, Aman, Harsh, Jasmit, Sandhya, Ajay Sharma, Namita, Suman, Pakhi, Priyanka, Mohit, Maithili, Abhishek, Satyam, Suraj, Rishika, Shrishiti, Antra, Mehak, Piyush, Kunal, Tushar, Mehak, Ridhima, Bhavika, Sachin, Mohd. Maaz towards media always inspires me too. My son Akshansh (B. B. A. IInd year student) also did some research work & of course Ishu who designed this book whole heartedly.

Lastly, I may conclude that It's a compliance of my own experience and research based upon the Internet and other books. It's a handy book for any student right from VI class to XII class. Even this book is very helpful for media students & who are interested to make their career in the field of media. I'm sure it is very useful for the students who are appearing in the media entrance test for BJMC too.

Surender Singh Dogra

(Author)

M:- 9811369585

Email:creativesworld@gmail.com

www.dwarkaparichay.com

www.creativesworldmediaacademy.com

Facebook link https://www.facebook.com/ssdogra

Linkedin link www.linkedin.com/in/ssdogra

contents

UNIT-III

UNIT-IV

You
Tube
digg
Bē

Introducion to Basic Media

Media & its Impact on Students life a very hot topic. Students should try to devote at least one hour daily (half an hour in the morning & half an hour before going to bed). They spare quality time in reading good books, inspiring/informative editorial/articles in newspaper which can enhance their vocabulary power & command over the language, watch good debate on TV, Film, listen good programmes aired on Radio, fair use of internet & Social media (Facebook, WhatsApp), the students can upgrade their knowledge about historical facts, achievements, National heros, become more responsive/extravert, more confident & able to get a better academics result. These tips can be very helpful for them to lay a sound foundation to qualify for media entrance exam, competition & face challenges more confidently & achieve what they want in their respective fields for a brighter career ahead.

UNIT-1

CHAPTER 1

Media can do Wonders in Studnets' Life

Media & its Impact on student's life. This is a very hot topic among the parents. Yes, it is an important issue of concern that Media has greater impact on students life. That's why most of the parents are worried about their ward's career. Parents don't want that their wards should spend too much time in watching Cricket Matches (which mostly telecast during examinations) movies, TV programmes mainly violent. Now, with the introduction of Smart Mobile phones, the excess use has become a headache for the parents.

To get rid of mobiles, C.B.S.E. took a very positive step towards it on 29th July, 2009 when a circular (Vide CBSE/AFF./CIRCULARS/2009) was served to all the affiliated schools of India by Joseph Emmanuel-Dy.Secretary (Affl.) C.B.S.E. As per the circular, the use of Mobile Phones definitely needs to be restricted in school environments. The Board is of the opinion that all stakeholders connected with school education such as students, parents, teachers and heads of institutes need to arrive at a consensus on the use of mobile phones in their schools and restricting its entry in the school campus. This is because mobile phones can be a serious cause of distraction, lack of concentration, anxiety, fear and sometimes even misuse. Even if the mobiles are on silent mode they can be a source of disturbance within the classroom as students can make use of Short Messaging Service (SMS)/what's app during the class or even during an assignment. The cameras which are a common feature now in most mobile phones can also be misused. The principal, teachers and other staff should also not be seen using the mobile in classrooms, playgrounds, common areas, laboratories and other parts of the school premises.

Yet, the use of smart mobile phone has tremendously increased in the student's life even in small villages & towns. Because this is really a wonderful device like Aladin-ka-Chirag (used in olden days story) which could bring everything you imagine. Undoubtedly, Smart Mobile phone has advance features to capture images, video, audio, text, SMS, radio FM, TV, porn sites, Facebook, Youtube, games, Music,What's app, thousands of apps etc. to communicate with anybody (known or unknown) across the world within a friction of second, its just a button away.

Media is called the 4th Estate of Democracy & it is really powerful. Actually, Media has the capability to influence opinions, behaviors, beliefes, attitudes and values among the mass. But, at present media, is known for negativity & criticized as misleading our new generation. The serious thing is that students are excessively surrounded by hundreds of TV Channels, Social Media option to keep themselves busy on their mobile & its application & sometimes they misuse it. There are many examples of it as there are very serious concern about our upcoming generation. The excessive use of Mobile & its distraction are deteriorating our Indian society to a large extent. But, the question is, whether we should keep away our wards from these gadgets or guide them to use this modern Media device more carefully to make it more meaningful with proper use of this useful & helpful gadget.

The students must utilize media to find out the solutions & update information of their interests. In a broader sense, it may be particularly related to their study, current news, information, subject query, career option, updates or happenings about their surrounding or nation which may be informative for their family, teachers, relatives, friends & connected colleagues. This is the best use of Media which is the need of the hour for our Next-Gen. As you know that our thought process is very much influenced & shaped by Media only. It means that our perception about any political party, social activity, corporate world, product, culture, public issue, local, national, international know how, art, culture, sports, public agenda etc. are all guided and influenced by the Media.

It is up to students, how they utilize their spare time in reading good books, inspiring/informative editorial/articles in newspaper which can enhance vocabulary & grab a good command on the language by watching good debates on TV, Film, listening good programmes aired on Radio by fair use of internet & Social media (Facebook, What's App), the students can upgrade their knowledge about historical facts, achievements, National hero, become more responsive/ extravert, become more confident & able to get better academic /practical result.

Students should manage to devote at least one hour daily (half an hour in the morning & half an before going to bed) in these Media resources during schooling. Because it can be very helpful for them to shape a sound foundation to qualify any entrance, competition & face challenges more confidently to achieve what they want to achieve in their respective fields for a brighter career option. By adopting the above suggestions, it's hundred percent sure that a student can become an asset for any nation. Yes, of course, Media can do wonders in Students' Life, if it's utilized well during their regular study.

CHAPTER 2

Writing Skill

We can find any word and use it. But writing an appropriate word or sentence comes with the experience and your vocabulary commond on a language. It's very important to know how to write and what to write about any person, place or anything around you using your imagination. When we start learning any language, we start to recognize the letters then words and after that sentences. This is the normal path to learn any language but command over a language comes through a lot of efforts. If it's your mother tongue than you can learn all these things quite easily but to understand another language you have to work hard to learn any other language. So, how can you get command over the other languages like English, Russian, Chinese, Japanese, Spanish, French, Korean, German or any other language of the world?

In almost all the states or UT's of India, English is taught right from the school level itself, most of the children also start learning Hindi particularly in northern & central part of India, the regional & local languages are also have their main source of communication. The question is that, how to master English or Hindi language so that you can express your views, thoughts or ideas among the masses.

Generally, when you come to the middle wing say VI class your teacher asks you to write an essay on Independence Day, Republic Day or My Best Friend. You can write anything but it is importantly to write good content. This is the beginning. If you really want to gain good writing skill, you should read good books, newspaper, magazines and go through contents available on the internet on any subject of your interest. Its also a fact that without a good reading habit you cannot develop good writing skills in your life. Reading and Writing go together. There are many writing skills and formats:

Message :

It should not be more than 10-20 words. It should be brief but to the point.

Like: India defeated Pak by 5 Wkts. In 1st ODI.

Caption:

Its generally used under a picture which explains the particular moment about the click, and it should not be more than15-20 words.

Ex. P.M. addressing the nation from the Red Fort.

Paragraph :

It should be around 250 words. It should be focusing on the subject so that maximum information can be gathered within the specified words limit.

Report :

The report of any event/incident/celebration/happening can be up to 500 words. It may contain the place, occasion, facts, significance, historical background, comments, opinions etc.

Script :

Script writing is yet another essential part of any play, drama, TV serials, documentary or a film. To write a good script you have to imagine & put your imagination into words to make your script more interesting.

Dialogue :

This is also used in drama, play, documentary, TV serials, or in a film to impress the audience in a more meaningful and interesting way.

Lyrics :

Folk songs are very popular in the Indian society till today. Moreover, in Hindi or regional languages, these lyrics or songs are the major attraction for the audiences who are always eager to hear in the movies.

Article/Editorial :

This is a very important part of any publication, because this is the backbone of any media house. Mostly, the senior editors/columnists/senior Journalists/experts in a particular field write these article as per their intellect & the reader's demand. It's written in a way to share their personal view on a particular topic. It may be of 500 words to quarter/half a page of the publication. It is published in the Editorial section where no photo is used to support the article or editorial in general. In the newspaper you'll find them in the middle of the newspapers or in the beginning of the magazines.

Feature article :

As the name suggests a feature article contains some important information, facts, figures, on any subject but with a few good photographs. So, if you are planning to write a feature article then you have to collect all the above mentioned information with some good pictures. The feature article may be prepared for half a page, full page or even two pages together. These feature articles are quite popular in the supplement pages of a newspaper or in magazines.

Interview :

This is yet another very popular format in the media to showcase an interview of a person. So, if you are willing to conduct an interview of any person or celebrity, you should be curious to collect maximum information from him/her. His/her early life, turning point, hobbies, passion, achievements, family or friends support, basic nature, role model, life style, devotion, ambition, etc. On the basis of all these tips, you will be able to showcase a good interview.

CHAPTER 3

Role of Social Media in the Modern World

Define Social Media.

Social media is an emerging new phenomenon which allows people to express their thought processes in an interactive manner on a real time basis using the Internet and its various technological advances.

"Social media consists of Internet sites where people can interact freely, sharing and discussing information about each other and their lives, using a multimedia mix of personal words, text, emo, animation, pictures, videos and audio."

Social media refers to the means of interaction among people in which they create, share, exchange information and ideas in virtual communities and networks. It differentiates from traditional/industrial media in many aspects such as quality, reach, frequency, usability, immediacy, and permanence.

Major features of SM

Social media differs from traditional/industrial media in many ways, including quality, reach, frequency, usability, immediacy, and permanence. At these Web sites, app individuals and groups create and exchange content and engage in person-to-person conversations. The major features of social media are as follows:

(a) It is easy to use.

(b) It allows you to become an instantaneous global generator, transmitter, publisher and broadcaster of data.

(c) It allows you to post your opinion on real time to the entire world.

(d) It allows you to interact with others on a real time basis. Profiles are often used as a point of contact between users.

(e) Social media uses audio, video, image or text on a variety of platforms for the purposes of facilitating instantaneous communication.

(f) A common feature in social applications is the use of live search results and filtering.

(g) Social networking sites aften have call-to-action-buttons that are supposed to motivate users to action.

Indian Information Technology Act, 2000

When one talks of social media, there is no regulatory/monitoring authority for the same. However, social media in India is regulated by the Indian Cyber Law under the Indian Information Technology Act, 2000. Advocate Pavan Duggal (well-known Cyber Law Expert) claims that social media service providers are intermediaries under Section 2(1)(w) of the Information Technology Act, 2000, wherein they are mandated to exercise due diligence while discharging their obligations under Section 79 of the Information Technology Act, 2000. Further, the Government of India has mandated various due diligences to be complied with by intermediaries including social media service providers as detailed under the Information Technology (Intermediary Guidelines) Rules, 2011. However, most of these compliances are of a proactive nature. There is no regulatory/monitoring authority for social media in India as of today. According to Advocate Pavan Duggal the Government has given the power to block undesirable content on social media to the Group Coordinator, Cyber Law Division, Ministry of Communications & Information Technology, Government of India. However before exercising such powers, the aforesaid legal entity must be satisfied that it is necessary to issue directions for interception or monitoring or decryption of information through any computer source in any of the following circumstances:

(a) In the interest of the sovereignty or integrity of India;

(b) In the interest of defense of India;

(c) In the interest of security of the State;

(d) In the interest of friendly relations with foreign states;

(e) In the interest of public order;

(f) In the interest of preventing incitement to the commission of any cognizable offence relating to the above; or

(g) For investigation of any offence.

Clearly, the aforesaid are broad parameters which have not been specifically defined.

Authenticity of SM A/c

There is No criteria/provision/restriction to open/create any FB-Page/A/c Website, twitter means anybody can do it even without any authenticity for others also. The law has not stipulated any specific provision/restriction to open/create any FB-Page/A/c. However, Section 66A is of relevance. If anybody opens the said account on social media which is primarily grossly offensive or menacing in character, the same itself becomes an offence under Section 66A of the Information Technology Act, 2000. However, the law really does not provide for any provision for authenticity of any FB-Page/A/c. The same is also the position for other social media websites. In fact, the Indian Cyber Law does not really either define social media by name nor does it define a category and also does not specifically refer to Facebook or Twitter or other social media platforms. However, certain restrictions are put on service providers providing social media platforms. Rule 3 of the Information Technology (Intermediary Guidelines) Rules, 2011 provides that intermediaries have to have rules and regulations, terms and conditions and privacy policy and inform the users of computer resource not to host, display, upload, modify, publish, transmit, update or share any information that —

(a) belongs to another person and to which the user does not have any right to;

(b) is grossly harmful, harassing, blasphemous, defamatory, obscene, pornographic, pedophilic, libelous, invasive of another's privacy, hateful, or racially, ethnically objectionable, disparaging, relating or encouraging money laundering or gambling, or otherwise unlawful in any manner whatever;

(c) harms minors in any way;

(d) infringes any patent, trademark, copyright or other proprietary rights;

(e) violates any law for the time being in force;

(f) deceives or misleads the addressee about the origin of such messages or communicates any information which is grossly offensive or menacing in nature;

(g) impersonate another person;

(h) contains software viruses or any other computer code, files or programs designed to interrupt, destroy or limit the functionality of any computer resource;

(i) threatens the unity, integrity, defence, security or sovereignty of India, friendly relations with foreign states, or public order or causes incitement to the commission of any cognizable offence or prevents investigation of any offence or is insulting any other nation.

Punishment for misusing

Advocate Pavan Duggal further added that posting of any filthy/unethical posts on social media is an offence under Section 66A of the amended Information Technology Act, 2000. This is a punishable offence with 3 years imprisonment and also with a fine. If any person uses any computer or communication device to communicate, send or transmitt any text, video, audio or image, for the various activities listed under Section 66A(a) to (c), he shall be guilty of an offence, which is punishable with imprisonment for a term which may extend to three years and with fine. Any person who sends, by means of his computers and communication devices, any information that is grossly offensive or has menacing character commits an offence under Section 66A of the amended Information Technology Act, 2000.

SM follows IIT Act

Currently, there is no specific law on social media.

However, since social media uses data and information in the electronic form, it is directly covered under the Indian Information Technology Act, 2000.

SM in Election:

There is tremendous future of use of social media in the upcoming elections. These elections will be the most techno-savvy elections that India has ever seen. There will be extensive use of social media by all candidates to address the concerns and issues of the internet community and netizens.

However the use pertaining to social media in India is evolving as time is passing by. Candidates should not expect social media to have a magic wand that social media could itself win elections. However, with the increased usage and dependence on social media including access to social media through mobile phones, social media will act as an important influencer influencing people to decision making capabilities for elections. Although, India needs to learn as to how the social media is being used in the US and how election authorities in the US are monitoring social media, today in India we do not have any mechanism to monitor social media. Social media will play an important role in the coming future although as of today it is not yet playing a predominant role in the elections because the number of users on social media is much less than the total number of electorate in the elections.

The Election Commission has reportedly issued the following instructions for the uses of social media:

"Candidates are required to file affidavits in Form-26 at the time of filing of nominations.

Para 3 of this Form requires that email ID of the candidate, if any, should be communicated to the Commission in this Form. The Commission finds it necessary that authentic social media accounts of candidates should also be informed to the Commission…

candidates and political parties shall include all expenditure on campaigning, including expenditure on advertisements on social media, both for maintaining a correct account of expenditure and for submitting the statement of expenditure. This, among other things, shall include payments made to internet companies and websites for carrying advertisements and also campaign related operational expenditure on making of creative development of content, operational expenditure on salaries and wages paid to the team of workers employed by such candidates and political parties to maintain their social media accounts, etc…the provisions of model code of conduct and related instructions of the Commission issued from time to time shall also apply to the content being posted on the internet, including social media websites, by candidates and political parties."

Who is held responsible for wrong postings:

Most of the candidates are today hiring IT experts for handling their social media activities. These, IT experts handle the said social media accounts for and on behalf of the said candidates. In the eyes of law, the said accounts belong to the said candidates and they alone shall be responsible for use or misuse or abuse of the said social media accounts.

SM is more effective than the old method of election campaigning.

Social media is distinctly effective in as much as it optimizes the use of technology. It may be viewed as a cost effective means to reach out to large sections of the electorate. As more and more Indian electorate is using the digital ecosystem as also mobile phones; social media becomes an important tool to address the said community through social media using mobiles and communication devices. Social media is more effective than the old method of election campaigning. However, given the fact that Internet penetration in the country is relatively still less and is growing with the passage of time, it is clear that social media will not replace the old method of election campaigning. On the contrary it will continue to be an effective and important added tool in the arsenal of the relevant election candidates that they go about their election campaigning for winning elections.

Precaution/guidelines using SM particularly during election campaign?

The following precautions/guidelines should be taken into consideration while using social media:

(1) It is advisable not to launch personal attacks while using social media.

(2) It is better to be duly diligent while using language and expressions on social media.

(3) During the course of election campaigning, the candidates should not do any of the following acts:

(i) swear or abuse somebody as the said swear words could be said to be grossly offensive. The same could also be said to be having menacing character and their act could come within the ambit of Section 66A(a) of the amended Indian Information Technology Act, 2000.

(ii) Anything defamatory which affects the character, reputation, standing or goodwill of a person could also be deemed to be grossly offensive.

(iii) Making false allegations against the character of a person or character assassination could also qualify as grossly offensive and having a menacing character.

(iv) Using insulting words or symbols which are obscene, could also qualify as grossly offensive and having a menacing character.

(v) Calling someone names could also be brought within the ambit of being grossly offensive or having a menacing character

(vi) Posting the picture of a person in uncomplimentary situations and environment could also be said to be grossly offensive or having menacing character. For example, if you morphed the photograph of a girl/boy's face in unwarranted situations, the same could be grossly offensive and having a menacing character.

(vii) Electronic morphing which shows a person depicted in a bad light could also be seen as an example of information being grossly offensive or having menacing character.

(viii) Using vernacular abuses or bad words in English could also qualify as grossly offensive or having menacing character.

(ix) Threatening somebody with consequences for his life, apart from being separate offences, could be also construed as information which is grossly offensive or having menacing character.

(x) Threatening to expose the ill-deeds of somebody could also qualify as information which has a menacing character.

(xi) Information containing malicious, mischievous character assassination

(xii) Information containing morphed pictures aimed at hurting religious sentiments.

(xiii) Information showing gods and goddesses of particular religions in an uncomplimentary light.

(xiv) Putting the picture of a person against a slogan/ phrase/saying which does not depict his true character or personality.

(xv) Deceiving the addressee or recipient about the origin of such messages. For example, sending emails from a fake email account to another person, could qualify as an offence under Section 66A of the amended Indian Information Technology Act, 2000.

(xvi) Further misleading the addressee or recipient about the origin of such messages, e.g. sending e-mails and SMSs in the name of an anonymous user could also be brought under Section 66A of the amended Indian Information Technology Act, 2000.

(xvii) E-mail containing fake recruitment offers to unsuspected members of the public, could also qualify as an offence under Section 66A of the amended Indian Information Technology Act, 2000.

(xviii) Maintain Privacy: Do not discuss a situation involving named or pictured individuals on a social media site without their permission.

(xix) Don't Use Pseudonyms: Never pretend to be someone else. Tracking tools enable supposedly anonymous posts to be traced back to their authors.

Economical & Effective for any social/political/business campaign

Social media is extremely useful for propaganda or for a big campaign. It is cost-effective and allows you to reach out to large sections of the Internet users and netizen community on the click of a button. Social media is extensively being used across the world for social/political/business campaigns.

The App World

Today is the world of App. Yes, no doubt about that there are more useful, practical apps that add versatility and utility in our day to day life. All the branches of Media like Radio, Television, Newspapers, magazines, film, music album, celebrities, web portal have created their own apps to interact with the mass.

Define App

Mobile app is an application software designed to run on mobile devices such as smart phones and tablet computers. Most such devices are sold with several apps bundled as pre-installed software, such as a web browser, email client, calendar, mapping program, and an app for buying music or other media or more apps.

Birth of App

They began appearing in 2008 and are typically operated by the owner of the mobile operating system, such as the Apple App Store, Google Play, Windows Phone Store, and BlackBerry App World.

Utility of Apps

Measurement tools and construction calculators, apps for adding flashlight functionality to your Android, first aid manuals, barcode scanners, and more. There are bunch of utility apps, ranging from the simple to the esoteric, that should help you get more practical utility out of your Android smart phone or tablet. Nowadays, these apps are very popular among the youths in particular. Because with the help of various apps you can easily find anything you want at your door step. If you want anything to eat, want to hire any taxi or auto, bus, train or air-ticket, metro train route map, distance or fare, functioning with financial institutions, for female security, medical assistance, you have to download the specific apps & able to get the maximum use of them that too without spending a single penny.

CHAPTER 4

Photography-The Soul of Media

Media, without image, is like a body without soul. Yes, its hundred percent true fact that photography plays very important role in the field of Media. Its not a matter of still or video, the Photography has its own impact in Media. So, let's understand what is photography and what are the basic tips taken into consideration while doing good photography. According to Sh. O.P. Sharma (who is legend in Indian Photography world) Oscar Barnic (Germany) has great contribution in the Photography field because he invented the Camera & that's why he is called the father of Photography. Sharma ji even claims that World Photography Day has been celebrating on 19th August since 1991 every years with his own IIPC'S efforts.

It is a fact that Photography is not only a a science but also an art. It becomes an art when a photographer takes the pains to explore the wells of creativity that are contained in photography. It becomes a science when the photographer concerns himself with the technical aspects that play a vital role while capturing the photographs. But at the same time creativity & capturing the moments matter a lot because it's the spirit which attract the viewers & appreciated by one & all. Because creativity with intellectuality in artistic view is the basic thumb rule of better photography.

This is mostly because, as an activity, a passion and a profession, photography cannot really be contained. The options or types or branches are really as endless as it can get. Make a pre planned move and read on to know more about the various types or branches of photography.

Indoor Photography

Let's start with Indoor photography that are taken in a room or studio. Indoor photography needs good reflector (flash) to get good photography results. Mostly, its like a studio photography where you can get your photograph which is generally used for job or ID card or for Passport purpose.

Aerial Photography

Aerial photography means those photographs that are shot from a plane, a helicopter, a hot-air balloon, drone or any other mode of airborne transportation.

Adventure Photography

Ever seen those photographs taken of bikes high in the air? Well, you can thank adventure photography for that. Adventure photography is all about photos of daring feats, climbing a mountain peak, sports and adventure in general.

Architectural Photography

Architectural photography involves that art or taking aesthetic photographs of properties that help promote the sale of the same.

Astrophotography

Astrophotography stands to signify space photography, or photography that materializes into the confines of reality with the assistance of a telescope.

Black & White Photography

Black and white photography deals with classic black and white shots that throw light on the expressions of people, places, destination.

Commercial Photography

Those pictures that are taken to promote products, services and companies come under the large banner of commercial photography. In other words, the photographs which can be helpful in advertising any products or services come under this category.

Event Photography

Event photography stands to represent the photographs taken of events that can involve concerts, festivals, parties, engagements, weddings, etc.

Forensic Photography

Photographs taken to help or solve a crime or work on clues are best described as forensic photography.

Fashion Photography

A photograph taken to promote or publicize fashion falls under the broad banner of fashion photography. Those glossy pictures you see in glossy fashion magazines of models are best examples of fashion photography.

Nature Photography

Nature photography brings within its folds the various photographs that are taken of birds, animals, plants, the sea, landscapes, fall, mountains, etc.

Sports Photography

Sports photography is the branch of photography that revolves around photographs taken of sport stars in their live playing action.

Underwater Photography

A photograph that is taken under water with the aid of a water-tight camera falls under the fascinating branch of underwater photography.

Monuments Photography

This is yet another very important branch of Photography called Monuments photography. The historical monuments like India Gate, Qutub Minar, Taj Mahal, Char Minar, Forts, comes under monuments photography category.

Major significance of photography in Media

The Light, angle, aperture, subject, object, close up, wide shots, speed, shutter, clicking moments etc. are very important parts to capture a good photograph. If you have passion, patience, creativity above all the ability to clicking the button on right moment than only a good photograph can be taken. All these above mentioned qualities make you an outstanding photographer. Single photograph can reveal the whole story of any incident that's why photography has greater impact or significance in the field of Media and it will remain forever.

CHAPTER 5

Radio means Infotainment

Radio is really the most economical media device in the world. Even a small villager can afford to buy it. The interesting thing is that Radio is the ultimate source of getting news, information & enjoy the entertainment programmes in any part of the world. The most interesting thing about Radio is that you can hear it even doing some other work.

Right from the Independence day or Republic Day Parade, Sports/Cricket commentary, Nowadays, 'Man Ki Baat' by our Prime Minister Sh.Narender Modi etc. are aired through Radio and a large population can listen popular programs at their own convenient places. That's why Radio is quite popular in India. Earlier it was Vividh Bharti, Aakashwani now the FM channels have improved the quality of voice and accessibility even to the interior part of rural India. With the internet revolution, the accessibility of Radio on Mobile has tremendously increased. Now, most of the radio stations are available online and they have even created their own App which can be downloaded from Google App store so that one can enjoy their programmes.

Inventor of Radio

But the question is who invented this wonderful device called Radio. Guglielmo Marconi an Italian inventor, first proved the feasibility of radio communication. He sent and received his first radio signal in Italy in 1895. By 1899 he flashed the first wireless signal across the English Channel and two years later received the letter "S", telegraphed from England to Newfoundland.

World Radio Day is celebrated on 13 February every year. World Radio Day is about celebrating radio, why we love it and why we need it today more than ever. A day to remember the unique power of radio which touch as lives and brings people together across every corner of the globe.

In India, Radio was the most popular source of news, information & entertainment up to 1980 because after that Television also attracted the Indian audiences. Some radio programmes are still in the memory of millions of radio listeners: Who can forget the sweet voice of Ameen Sayani 'Binaca Geet Mala' aired on Radio Ceylon. The commentary of Jasdev Singh from Red Fort, cricket commentary of Sushil Doshi, Britania Quiz, Radio Najibabad, Yuvvani-Mahfil, Yadon ke Jharokhe se etc. were full of information, relays from far off places & entertainment.

Nowadays, most of the radio stations, are aired with spiritual & motivational programmes in the morning schedule. After that old & new film songs, daily updates, current topics, event update, inspiring interviews, Educational updates, sports, art, cultural, socio-political, religious updates are also main attractions aired on different radio stations that attract audiences.

'Suhana Safar' with Annu Kapur aired on 92.7 FM is quite popular among the music lovers. Annu Kapur presents very interesting anecdotes about the film artists & even director/writer and clubbed with old melodious songs. Soul yatra, with life coach Sharat, is a very motivational & inspiring program aired Every week - Monday to Friday @ FM 104, News bulletins on FM Gold at 106.4 after every hour, is enjoyed daily by millions of radio listeners.

Main Indian Radio Station in India are :

All India Radio, RadioCity 91.1 FM, RADIOINDIGO 91.9 FM, BIG FM 92.7FM, RED 93.5 FM, MYFM 94.3FM, RADIO ONE 94.3 FM, HIT 95 FM, RADIO MIRCHI 98.3 FM, 101.1 FM, AIR FM GOLD 102.3, 102.6 FM, FEVER 104 FM, 104.8FM, 106.2 FM, FM GOLD 106.4 FM

FM GOLD

FM Gold Channel came on air on 1st September, 2001. Broadcast from AIR Delhi as a niche infotainment channel, it has 30% News and Current affairs component and 70% entertainment programming. FM Gold can be heard in all the four Metros, i.e. Delhi, Mumbai, Kolkata and Chennai.

Community Radio: With the introduction of Community Radio, the accessibility of Radio has increased tremendously even at the grass root level. The main advantage of Community Radio is to able to listen radio even where the main radio station signals are unapproachable, local languages, local art, culture &

recognition is easily accessible and promoted through it. These Community radio are very popular in different parts of India.

Online Radio

Awaz 107.2 is a Hindi FM Radio channel which provides Live Streaming Online. One can to listen more than 80 Hindi FM Radio Stations Online. Live Streaming Hindi Music can be enjoyed 24 by 7. If you want to listen this from mobile device it can be downloaded.

This FM serves the Asian and African population in Glasgow, broadcasting in English, Urdu, Punjabi, Hindi, Paharhi and Swahili delivering entertainment, news and local, national and community information.It also covers particular faiths Christianity, Hinduism, Sikhism and Islam.

www. awazfm.co.uk

Free Internet Radio Stations Online

http://www.onlineradios.in/

http://www.moviebuffer.com

Popular Foreign Radio Stations in India:

When India got independence, **BBC Radio Station** was the first choice of Indian Radio listeners. BBC radio station was also the main source of world news for the Indian up to 1980. This radio provides English & Hindi news service which is still very popular in Indian community.

Radio Ceylon launched the Hindi Service of the station in the early 1950s. Bollywood star Sunil Dutt & King of Radio Voice Ameen Sayani got a lot of popularity through this radio station only. The broadcast of Binaca / Cibaca Geetmala and "Lipton Ke Sitaare." Were quite liked by the Indians in the late 60's.

Radio Nepal is also quite popular among the Himalayan states of India. The broadcast of Hindi movie songs & news are still of the main interest for Indians.

Now, in the age of digital world, the FM radio stations are becoming more & more popular. They are easily accessible even on a simple Mobile device. So, we can say that Radio has become the pulse of the whole Indian community. That's why Radio is called the Ultimate Source of Information & Entertainment.

UNIT-2

CHAPTER 1

Media Literacy

Introduction:
MEDIA:

The word **media** comes from the Latin plural of medium.
Medium: The means of communication, as radio and television, newspaper, magazines, films & internet that reach or influence people widely.

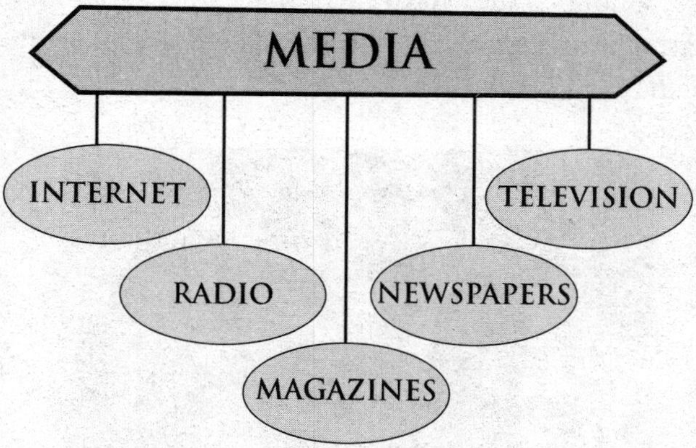

(Figure-1: Sources of Media in our day to day life)

Watch TV & read Newspaper for news, Radio(FM) for entertainment.

Visit Website & apps to check out the latest trends & shopping.

Make friends & communicate with other people or community, Through mailer, social media (Facebook, WhatsAap, Tweet opinion, Linkedin etc.)

Where we can share our opinion, information, upload videos & photos.

It means media is omnipresent. We all are surrounded by it in our routine life.

Nowadays, media has created greater impact on the whole society. Media is able to influence our opinion, action, reaction, perceptions about the world around us. Our thought process is very much influenced & shaped by media only. Its means that our perception about any political party, social activity, corporate world, product, culture, public issue, local, national, international know how, art, culture, sports, public agenda etc. are all created by the media.

P.M. Visit to Foreign countries,

Public issues: Reservation,

FMCG product of Baba Ram Dev.

(Figure 2 Internet-Social Media)

Media Literacy

As a citizen & media practitioners it is essential for us to understand the basic ethics & aspects of media like ownership, agenda and interest so that we are able to serve it with transparently, honestly, neutral & justify manner. This awareness of media is called Media Literacy.

National Association for Media Literacy Education, NJ, USA Define Media Literacy

"Media literacy empowers people to be both critical thinkers and creative producers of an increasingly wide range of messages using image, language, and sound. It is the skillful application of literacy skills to media and technology messages."

In USA, Media Literacy Week is celebrated to highlight the power of media literacy education and its essential role in education today.

Impact of Media

The 4 pillars of Democracy are-

1. Executive (Government)
2. Legislature (Parliament & State Assemblies, etc)
3. Judiciary (Supreme Court, High Court & Other Judicial centres)
4. Media (Newspaper, Internet, Blogs & whatever which expresses people's aspirations)

Good Contribution of 4 pillars are equally important for successful democratic countries

Media is called the 4th estate of Democracy & it is really powerful. Actually, Media has the capability to influence opinions, behaviors, believes, attitudes and values among the mass.

Mass Media

Media which can influence maximum number of people, so it is called Mass Media.

Main content forms of Media:

Apart from the main branches of Media mentioned above, the following are also important parts of Media:

Advertising, Books, Music, Theatre, Play, Feature Films, Fiction/Non-Fiction, Entertainment, News, Website, Social Media

Media Studies

It is the study of media is composed of and how it affects the people. It comprises vast study of communication, history, politics, design, information, economics, sociology, literature, film, photography, philosophy etc.

Key concepts in Media Studies are:

a) Media Audiences- who are targeted

b) Media Technology-Process of production

c) Media Agencies/Ownership-Producer

d) Media language-How to convey in different domain

e) Media Categories-print, radio, TV, films, internet etc.

f) Media Representation-How to showcase with different media options.

Activity

(Just watch TV for 30 minutes & note down the advertisement that during this period and write down the answer to the above mentioned questions)

Key Concepts in Studying the Media

Media means the concept of Mass, be it mass society, mass culture, mass media or mass audiences. It is entirely different from earlier days or traditional society.

Importance of Traditional Methods

Traditional Society

As the name suggests it is a community based society, like a small village/town where everyone knows each other.

Traditional Culture

The cultural values & ideas shared by a community is called Traditional Culture.

Traditional media for transmission of message:

Stories, song, dance, philosophy, drama, myths, legends were the main sources to transmit the messages among the mass. For example Akbar-Birbal ke kisse, Dadi maa ke Nushkhe/kahaniyan, folk songs/dances etc.

Define Mass

Mass means involving or affecting large number of people or things

"Mass Communication" & "Mass Media" term got recognition only after World War I(1914-1919) . Many movements like Russian Revolution, The Indian Independence Movement, the Trade Union Movement were the main forces behind Mass. The media owners realized the power of mass media and it came into existence in 1930.

Mass Society (Social relationship)

Mass Culture (Some cultural followers)

Mass Media

Media like radio, TV, newspaper which can influence mass rather than a particular group or a community is called Mass Media.

Comparison between Folk (traditional) & Mass Culture

A single shopkeeper & introduction of Macdonald in 1957.

Mass Media Technologies

With the invention & adaptability of new technologies, the accessibility of Media increased tremendously.

Mass Audience

As a result of that the Mass Audience came across media.

Audience Theories

How audience respond or react to the media message is called Audience Theories.

Hypodermic Theory or Magic Bullet Theory

According to this theory, Media is influential & has direct effect on audience.

(Exp.Activity: Independence Movement, 1984 Riots)

Propaganda:

Being unacceptable or evil in nature (Negative approach)

1. Political Propaganda
2. Subtle Propaganda

The Two Step Model

In a world, there was only one media source which was completely under the control of one interested party, the Hypodermic Theory or the Magic Bullet theory.

Media Ownership-Conglomerates (big companies) & its ethics or essentials.

Media Representation:

It is an important issue in Media Literacy. Representation means speech or writing, photo or video & its credibility to showcase the mass.

Representation of Rural Issues

1. Agriculture issue

2. Education

3. Employment

4. Basic amenties

Representation of Minorities

Religious

SC/ST/OBC Quota

Technical Codes used as in Media

Music, Sound Effect, Camera angles & Editing.

Question Bank 1

1. What is Media?
2. What are the branches of Media?
3. How Media has influence our day to day life?
4. What is Media Literacy?
5. Define Media Literacy?
6. Why is Media powerful?
7. What is Mass Media?
8. Name other forms of Media?
9. What is Media Studies?
10. What are the key concepts in Media Studies?
11. What is Traditional Media?
12. What is Traditional Culture?
13. Define Mass.
14. Propaganda
15. Media Ownership & its representation
16. Representation of Rural Issues
17. Technical Codes used in Media

CHAPTER 2

The Film Language

MISE EN SCENE French Term means 'to put into scene' or 'staging an action'.

The composition or film making includes the following elements:

Production Design

Set, Location, Actors & their movements, Costumes,Make up, Sound, Shot composition , Lighting.

The importance of a film in the mass society.

It's a medium of entertainment to give a message among mass-larger impact on society.

Activity:

Visit to Financial institution/Post office Prepare a chart/ PPT/Documentary to showcase their infrastructure & functioning.

What kind from of ground plan is required For a film?

Activity

A diagrammatic representation of how the setting looks like in a scene.

Plan a stage with imagination & creativity clubbed together.

Create an environment in Classroom activities to make a film.

Producer, Director, Artists, Script, Design, Theme, Editor, Coordinator, Shots & composition of sets, Camera

Question Bank 2

1. What is Film?
2. Name the Composition of Film making elements?
3. What is the importance of Film?
4. What is a ground plan to make a Film?

CHAPTER 3

The Television World

Television as a Medium: The understanding of the specific nature of television as medium. The nature of the content of the various programmes made for the television.

Define Television

An electronic item that update everyone through news bulletins, discussions, live match coverage about what is happening in your & other societies. Its very effective medium for individual & family entertainment. It can be seen millions of all age group people beyond any boundaries.

Tele is a Greek word means Far & Vision is a Latin word means to see

So, Television means you can see the event or happening far from at your home.

Television or TV is a telecommunication medium used for transmitting sound with moving images in monochrome (B & W), or in color, and in two or three dimensions. Television is a mass medium, for entertainment, education, news and advertising.

Television in India is a huge industry which has

thousands of programmes in many languages. The small screen has produced numerous celebritie, out of which, a few attain national fame. More than half of all Indian households own a television. As of 2012, the country has a collection of over 823 channels of which 184 are paid channels. The regular daily transmission started in 1965 as a part of All India Radio.

National telecasts were introduced in 1982. In the same year, colour TV was introduced in the Indian market. Indian small screen programming started off in the early 1980s. At that time there was only one national channel Doordarshan, which was government owned. Hum Log-the first soap opera a family serial was the first serial which got lot of popularity in India. The Mahabharata & Ramayana both Indian spiritual & mythological stories were the first major television serials produced.

Comparison between TV & Cinema

Nature of TV Production & Consumption

TV has the capacity for production as well as distribution of the programmes at mass level.

The structure of TV industry revolves around 3 parts:

1. The clients (the channels like NDTV, Aaj Tak, DD)
2. The Producers
3. The Sponsors (the various advertisers)

Soap Opera

In India Hum Log in, 1984 was written by Manohar Shyam Joshi directed by P.Kumar Vasudev

Maggi hit adversiters

156 episodes in seventeen months.

Culture of Music based programmes.

Chitrahar during 70 era on TV is the best example. Superhit Muqabla was yet another popular programmes for several years during 90's.

Some of the Music based Channels

MTV was the first kind of such channel, V Channel, B4u, 9XM is India's No. 1 Hindi Film Music Channel owned by 9X Media.

Educational TV, Non-Fiction on TV

Television came to New Delhi, India on 15th Sept., 1959 as the National Television Network of India. In India television has been an efficient tool for imparting education to primary, secondary & university level students.

Important efforts are mentioned below:

1. Secondary School Television Project (1961)to teach XI class students
2. Krishi Darshan (1966)-A project of Delhi Agriculture Television
3. IGNOU- DD telecast 1991 programs for distance learning!.
4. Gyan Darshan Educational Channel in 2000.

Non-fiction shows on TV.

They are ranging from serious news & current affairs broadcast to programmes that are purely entertaining.

Documentary is defined as a nonfiction report that devotes its full time slot on one thesis or subject, usually under the guidance of single produced. These documentaries on Doordarshan have been quite frequent, at times borrowing several titles from Film Division of

India for telecast. They have been mostly biographies of personalities, and some have been made specially as Television Documentaries on current affairs or events, mostly providing the official point of view to issues of national concern.

Reality TV Show

Documentaries and non fictional programmes such as news & sports are usually not classified as reality shows.

Big Brother(of UK like Big Boss in India) .

Reality television frequently portrays a modified & highly influenced form of reality, utilizing sensationalism to attract viewers & so to generate advertising profits. Tol mol ke bol, KBC etc.

Question Bank 3

1. Define Television?
2. Name three parts of TV Industry.
3. What is educational TV programme?
4. What is non-fiction TV shows?
5. What is reality TV show?

CHAPTER 4

The Print World

Define Print Media

Whole range of media which makes use of printing machines to make multiple copies is called Print Media.

Gernam fellow Johann Gutenberg invented the printing press in the 1450, and the first book to ever be printed was a Latin language Bible, printed in Mainz, Germany.

Leaflets, pamphlets and books were the earliest Print Media. But by the late 17th Century,

Poster of films and hoardings were also a part of Print Media.

Newspaper & periodicals published regularly in the European countries.

The news of all kinds in the media is known as the Press & the professional writers who write are called Journalist and this profession is called Journalism.

Define News

News is the written, audio or visual information about an event, a happening. Presentation or representation or construction of an event is called news.

"Wherever you move, there is a news

Its up to you, how you view"

आप जहाँ कहीं भी होते हैं वहां चारों तरफ ख़बरें हैं लेकिन ये आप पर निर्भर करता हैं आप उसे किस नजरिए से देखते-समझते हैं।

What is Journalism

Mainstream journalism treats news as a commodity to be bought & sold in the market.

What are the main formats of a newspaper

1. "Broadsheet"(Quality or Serious) Press-The Hindustan Times, The Indian Express etc.
2. "Tabloid" or "Yellow Journalism" (Popular or

Sensational) Press-Midday, Mumbai Mirror, Sandhya Times, etc.(Famous people, crime, public corruption, sex etc.)

3. "Berliner"-It's a little narrower & shorter than the broadsheet & slightly taller & wider than the tabloid. The Guardian, Mint etc. (containing quality & serious journalism)

Contents & Layout of a newspaper

There are some important formats that comes under news such as feature, editorials and columns etc.

1. News stories, advertisements
2. Lead or main news story for front page of a newspaper
3. Source of the news story (Reporter or News Agency etc.)
4. City news or local news, followed by National or regional pages,
5. Editorial page-Articles, Column of Editor, Letter to the editor etc.
6. International News (Source from AP, Reuter,AFP etc.)
7. Business, Sports Pages
8. Classified Advertisements (corporate, industrial, consumer, tenders, notices, real estate ads etc.)
9. Entertainment Page-Film, TV, Glamour
10. Supplements

"Tabloid television" is the reflection of the Tabloid Press.

Basic elements of a newspaper:

photographs, cartoons, tables, advertisements, infographics, etc.

Journalese-is a term which means the language of Journalism.

Question Bank 4

1. What is print media?
2. Define news.
3. Define journalism.
4. What are the main formats of newspaper?
5. What are contents & layout in a newspaper?

CHAPTER 5

The Radio World

Inventor of Radio

Guglielmo Marconi an Italian invented, the radio communication. He sent and received his first radio signal in Italy in 1895. By 1899 he flashed the first wireless signal across the English Channel and two years later received the letter "S", telegraphed from England to Newfoundland.

World Radio Day is, celebrated on 13 February every year. World radio day is about celebrating radio, why we love it and why we need it today more than enything. A day to remember the unique power of radio, to touch lives and to bring people together across every corner of the globe.

Radio programmes can be classified into two major categories:

1. Spoken Word Programme- News bulletins, talks, discussion, interviews, educational programmes, targeted audience programmes directed at children, women, rural/urban listeners, quizzes, talk shows, radio plays, radio feature & documentaries.
2. Music Programmes-All kinds of musical performances-instrumental or non-instrumental (classical, semi classical, popular), jocky programmes, film songs & variety programmes.

3. Drama, features & documentaries requires both the spoken words & the music. These popular programmes are aired on FM stations, AIR & Vividh Bharti.

In India, Radio was the most popular source of news, information & entertainment up till 1980 because after that Television also attracted the Indian audiences. Some radio programmes are still in the memory of millions of radio listeners: who can forget the sweet voice of Ameen Sayani Binaca Geet Mala aired on Radio Cylone. The commentary of Jasdev Singh from Red Fort, cricket commentary of Sushil Doshi, Britania Quiz, Radio Najibabad, Yuvvani-Mahfil, Yadon ke Jharokhe se etc. were full of information, live moment from far places & entertainment.

Nowadays, on most of the radio stations, the Spiritual & Motivational programmes are aired in the morning schedule. After that old & new film songs, daily updates, current topic, event update, inspiring interviews, educational updates, sports, art, cultural, socio-political, religious updates are also main attractions aired on different radio stations that attracts audiences.

Suhana Safar with Annu Kapur aired on 92.7 FM is quite popular among the music lovers. Annu Kapur even presents very interesting story about the of film artists & even directors/writers and club it with old melodious songs. Soul yatra with life coach Sharat is a very motivational & inspiring programme aired every week from - Monday to Friday - Started on 7th Sept 2015 - 06.00 am to 07.00 am @ FM 104 News bulletin, on FM Gold at 106.4 after every hour, is listened daily by millions of radio listeners.

Main Radio Stations in India are :

All India Radio, RadioCity 91.1 FM, RADIOINDIGO

91.9 FM, BIG FM 92.7FM, RED 93.5 FM, MYFM 94.3FM, RADIO ONE 94.3 FM, HIT 95 FM, RADIO MIRCHI 98.3 FM, 101.1 FM, AIR FM GOLD 102.3, 102.6 FM, FEVER 104 FM, 104.8, 106.2 FM, FM GOLD 106.4 FM

FM GOLD

FM Gold Channel came on air on 1st September, 2001. Broadcast from AIR Delhi as a niche infotainment channel, it has 30% News and Current affairs component and 70% entertainment programming. FM Gold is available in the four Metros i.e. Delhi, Mumbai, Kolkata and Chennai.

Community Radio: With the introduction of Community Radio, the accessibility of Radio has increased tremendously even at the grass root level. The main advantage of Community Radio is to listen radio even where the main radio station signals are unapproachable, local languages, local art, culture & recognition is easily accessible promoted through it. These Community radio are very popular in different parts of small city and univercity campuses of India.

Online Radio

Awaz 107.2 Hindi FM Radio Live Streaming Online. Listen more than 80 Hindi FM Radio Stations Online.Enjoy Live Streaming Hindi Music 24 by 7. If You want to listen this from mobile device

This FM serves the Asian and African population in Glasgow, broadcasting in English, Urdu, Punjabi, Hindi, Paharhi and Swahili delivering entertainment, news local, national and community information.It also covers particular faiths Christianity, Hinduism, Sikhism and Islam. www. awazfm.co.uk

FREE INTERNET RADIO STATIONS ONLINE

http://www.onlineradios.in/

http://www.moviebuffer.com

Popular Foreign Radio Stations in India:

When India got independence, **BBC Radio Station** was the first choice of Indian Radio listeners. BBC radio station was also the main source of world news for the Indian up to 1980. This radio has English & Hindi news service which is still very popular in Indian community.

Radio Ceylon launched the Hindi Service of the station in the early 1950s. Bollywood star Sunil Dutt & King of Radio Voice Ameen Sayani got lot of popularity through this radio station only. The broadcast of Binaca / Cibaca Geetmala) and "Lipton Ke Sitaare." Were very much like by the Indians in late 60's.

Radio Nepal *is also quite popular among Himalayan states of India. The broadcast of Hindi movies songs & news are still the main interest for Indians.*

Now, in the age of digitations world, the FM radio stations are becoming more & more popular. They are easily accessible even on simple Mobile device itself. So, we can say that Radio has become the pulse of the whole Indian community. That's why Radio is called Ultimate Source of Information & Entertainment. The Radio programmes can be caterarised as follows.

News Bulletin: AIR aired news bulletins after every hour for five minutes. These news bulletins are not allowed on private FM radio stations, but they can transmit traffic, sports & weather news.

Newsreels: It presents spot reports, interview,

comments, extract from speeches etc. For a duration of 15 minutes. It an expensive format & needs skilled tape editing and well written narration.

Documentaries/Radio Features: It a technique of talks drama clubbed together narrate story of an event (past, present or future), biography of a great leader or an event of social, political, economic or cultural significance.

Radio Plays: These like are stage drama told through sound only (30 to 60 minutes). The voice of every character should be natural and distinguishable, justified to the character and of course delivered in an interesting style. (Fielden-the first Controller/Director General of AIR, introduced the present norms of 30 minutes radio play on AIR).

Talks: Radio talks are like chats with a friend who cann't see you and it should be impressive enough that the speaker is addressing him alone in an interesting and informative way.

Music Programmes: These are more popular than any other programme aired on Radio.

Movie Trailers: These are sponsored programmes aired on Vividh Bharti (15-30 minutes) in which names of stars,Producers, director, playback singers & musicians are mentioned majorly in the trailors.

Quizzes: Bournvita's Quiz Contest aired on Radio Ceylon is considered the best ever quiz contest aired on Radio.

Live Coverage/Running Commentary: This includes live coverage of national/international events. How can we forget the voice of Jasdev Singh -26th Republic day Parade live commentary from India Gate or Sushil Doshi-Cricket live commentary from a far away stadium.

Content Analysis: As radio is an entirely different type of audible medium, so content analysis means what listeners respond to and interpret the text.

Question Bank 5

1. Who invented Radio?
2. When Radio Day is celebrated?
3. How Radio programmes can be categorised?
4. What is Community Radio?
5. What is online Radio?

CHAPTER 6

The Internet World

With the invention of Internet, everyone gets the global accessibility easily that too only a click of button away. Internet is the greatest revolution in the field of communication & disseminating information from any part of the world within fracion of seconds.

The Internet came into existence with the development of electronic computers in the 1950s in several computer science laboratories in the United States, United Kingdom, and France with the development of the ARPANET (which would become the first network to use the internet Protocol-IP). The first message was sent over the ARPANET from computer science Professor Leonard Kleinrock's laboratory at University of California, Los Angeles (UCLA) to the second network node at Stanford Research Institute (SRI).

Packet switching networks such as ARPANET, NPL, Tymnet and Telenet were developed in the late 1960s and early 1970s using a variety of communication protocols. Donald Davies was the first to put theory into practice by designing a packet-switched network at the National Physics Laboratory in the UK, the first of its kind in the world and the cornerstone for UK research for almost two decades. Following, ARPANET further led to the development of protocols for Internetworking, in which multiple separate networks could be joined into a network of networks.

Access to the ARPANET was expanded in 1981. In 1982, the internet protocol suite (TCP/IP) was introduced as the standard networking protocol on the ARPANET.

In the 1980s, the work of British computer scientist Tim Berners-Lee on the World Wide Web theorized protocols linking hypertext documents into a working system, marking the beginning of the modern Internet.Since the mid-1990s, the Internet has had a revolutionary impact on culture and commerce, including the rise of near-instant communication with its discussion forums, blogs, social networking and online shopping sites. Increasing amounts of data are transmitted at higher and higher speeds over fiber optic networks. The Internet's takeover of the global communication landscape was almost instant in historical terms: it only communicated 1% of the information flowing through two-way telecommunication networks in the year 1993, already 51% by 2000, and more than 97% of the telecommunicated information was transmitted by 2007. Today the Internet continues to grow, driven by ever greater amounts of online information, commerce entertainment, and social networking. The interweaving of these networks is known as Internet.

The Fundamental Rings of Internet:

1. Sending layer-addresses and sends data
2. Data passes through-Middle layer
3. Cloud-Vodafone, BSNL, Airtel, Tata, MTNL, Yahoo, gmail, hotmail etc.

Data Transmission Process

This is an important part of Internet protocol(IP) structure, allowing each internet transmission to be identified with its unique packet ID. The IP allows packets being received to be collected into a buffer before it is revealed to the user. Its also transforming every culture with the access to the internet and putting everyone within immediate reach of everyone else.

Open Source

Google or Wikipedia have become the open source for public awareness can be accessed with the help of internet only.

Multicast and Unicast

Radio, television and satellite transmission-is referred as Multicast or one way communication. Information is transmitted From a single sending source to an unlimited number of receivers. But Internet's primary transmission method is 'unicast,' referring to being interactive, or two way communication. Unicast's IP includes the sender's assurance that the transmission is received.

Internet-Utility and its future

Internet has become the life line of the people. Internet is extensively used in every fields like, communication, business, relationship, media, education, health, sports, entertainment etc.

Website –Through the website of any organization or company we are able to get a lot of information about them without moving or spending time and money. So, website is a wonderful platform to explore many ideas and facts. Its a very helpful tool for a business, education, corporate etc.

Social Networking website: The social networking websites like orkut, linkedin, Whatsup & facebook have become very popular in the world. They offer many options to share contents, views, news, photos, videos, ideas, play games, interact with new people and expantd the networking world and business.

Blogs: Blogs are websites or parts of them maintained by individuals. Here various audio-visuals are shared with the audience & blogs are extensively used by the academician, scholars, politicians, social workers etc. for communicating their thoughts and achievements publicly with more accessibility.

Question Bank 6

1. What is I. P.?
2. What is the full form of w.w.w.?
3. What are the fundamental rings of Internet?
4. What is social networking website?
5. What is blog?

UNIT-3

CHAPTER 1

The Cinema World

The Cinema came into existence in the year 1895. Johann Zahn designed the first camera in 1685. But the first photograph was clicked by Joseph Nicephore Niepce in the year 1814.

The first camera was invented by Alexander Wolcott & patented on 8 may, 1840. It was Joseph Nicephore Niepce who used a sliding wooden box to take photographs.

Thomas Alva Edison assisted by his assistant Dickson succeeded in making a motion picture camera and set up a studio called the Black Maria Studio in 1880.

The history of film began in the 1890s, when motion picture cameras were invented and film production companies started to be established. Due to the limits of technology, films of the 1890s were under a minute long and until 1927 motion pictures were produced without sound.

The world's first film maker and presenter were Louis Lumiere and August Lumiere of France. The first ever show of cinema called Lumiere programme was held by Lumiere brothers at Café Grand, Paris, France on 28th December,1895.

Following the screening of the Lumiere moving pictures in London (1895), cinema became a sensation across Europe and by July 1896 the Lumière films had been in show in Bombay (now Mumbai). In the next year a film presentation by one Professor Stevenson featured a stage show at Calcutta's Star Theatre. With Stevenson's encouragement and camera, Hiralal Sen, an Indian photographer, made a film of scenes from that show, namely The Flower of Persia (1898).

The Ciname

Cinema is called the Cindrella of All Arts. Its is majorly divided into two eras:

1. The Silent Era (1895-1927)
2. The Sound Era (1927- till today)

Hollywood

Hollywood was a small community in 1870 and was incorporated as a municipality in 1903. It officially merged with the city of Los Angeles in 1910, and soon thereafter a prominent film industry began to flourish, its known as the most recognized film industry in the world.

By 1912, major motion-picture companies had set up production near or in Los Angeles. Hollywood became fsmoud the Tinseltown because of the glittering image of the movie industry. Its place as the home of the U.S. film industry, including several of its historic studios. Hollywood has since become a major center for film study in the United States of America.

Popularity in Soviet Union (USSR)

After the October Revolution of 1917, USSR was mainly an agrarian country spread over a vast area. Literacy rate very low in the entire nation. In that situation cinema became the ideal medium to reach out to the masses. Since Cinema plays directly on the senses of human beings, it could be understood by the illiterates, who lived in the remote areas. That's why Lenin remarked, "Cinema is the most important of all arts." Lev Kuleshov was the first scientist-cum-film-maker of cinema. Segei Eisenstein,

V.I. Pudovkin, Dziga vertov, Dovzhenko were the master filmmakers of Soviet Union.

Cinema is the most important of all arts.

Germany Cinema

After the Great October Revolution of Russia in 1917, Germans were recovering from a shattering defeat in the World War I (1914-1918). Most films were made show casing the realities happened which in Germany at that time.

Creativity with Actuality

The non-fiction films, later to be called and articulated as documentaries some into being in Europe. Joris Ivens in Netherlands, Walter in Germany and Dziga Vertov in USSR pioneered a kind of film that had nothing do with fiction but creativity showing actuality.

John Grierson (UK) called the work of Flaherty as 'creative treatment of actuality'. He raised several social issues like rights of women and workers. John is known as the pioneer for the cause of documentaries for his life long dedicated work. 'Real people' 'real issues' were the main focus for him. He wrote and lectured about cinema and documentaries through-out his life and trained many filmmakers and this unique idea.

The Sound Era-1927

Warner Brothers of USA produced the first sound film in the world in 1927. "The Jazz Singer" film in which a famous black singer Al Johnson was acting and singing. With the introduction of sound, many things in films, were attered dialogue became the source of information and even continuity. Documentary, political propaganda film and the musical were new exciting forms. Heightened speech, songs and dances found their space in the films with more interesting version. On the whole, the pace of editing, and the concept of rhythm changed. It was the beginning of a new epoch in Cinema.

Types/Kinds of Cinema in Hollywood

The most important development of Sound era was the development of Genres(Types/Kinds) in Hollywood. Comedy, Detective, Musical, Gangster, Western emerged as the main genres of American Cinema. Hollywood films are globally known for American life-style, beliefs and values. The international famous cinema award like Oscar are considered the most prestigious/highest award in the glamour world of cinema.

Oscars Award

The **Academy Awards, or "Oscars",** is an annual American awards ceremony hosted by the Academy of Motion Picture Arts & Sciences (A.M.P.A.S.) to recognize excellence in cinematic achievements in the United States film industry as assessed by the Academy's voting membership. The various category winners are awarded a copy of a statuette, officially called the Academy Award of Merit, which has become commonly known by its nickname "Oscar". The awards, first presented in 1929 at the Hollywood Roosevelt Hotel, are overseen by A.M.P.A.S.

The awards ceremony was first broadcast on radio in 1930 and televised in 1953. It is now seen live in more than 200 countries and can be streamed live online. The Oscars is the oldest entertainment awards ceremony; its equivalents, the Emmy Award for television, the Tony Awards for theatre, and the Grammy Awards for music and recording, are modeled after the Academy Awards. The 88th Academy Awards ceremony was held at the Dolby Theatre on February 28, 2016. A total of 2,947 Oscars have been awarded since the inception of the award.

Three Schools of the World in the Film History

The German Expressionism, Soviet Socialist Realism & Italina Neorealism are considered the three major schools of the world in the film history.

What is Neorealism

A movement called Neorealism emerged in Italy during the World War II and the fall of fascism. Popular Italian Cinema in 1940 wholly presented super rich, luxurious life of character and entirely hid the real life. These films were called "White telephone films." Roberto Rossellini presented his film Rome, Open City (1945) which was base on real life event during the last days of the fascist and Nazi occupation by Italy. Luchino Visconti made "La Terra Trema" (The Earth Trembles) in 1948 which was shot in Aci Trezza, a small fishing village on the east coast of Sicily, Italy. "Bicycle Thieves" made by Vittorio De Sica in 1948 was a story of a common man Antonio Ricci working as a casual labourer to earn his bread for the family. This film was appreciated across the world.

The Decade of Classical Cinema (1950-1960)

The period between World War II and the beginning

of the Nuclear Age, brought a different consciousness to the intellectuals globally. The practice of subtitling, para dubbing and holding international film festivals made the viewing of relations films at a common platform where people and filmmakers across cultural exchange came together and strengthened. The dominant filmmakers of this decades were : Robert Bresson, Jean Renoir(France), Satyajit Ray(India), Ingmar Bergman (Sweden), Mic healangelo Antonioni, Federico Fellini (Italy) and Akira Kurosawa (Japan).

Hollywood Cinema made the transition to colour & invented new formats like Widescreen to influence the television viewership. The better option/implementation of films, color, image, lenses and lighting equipment were utilized during this decade.

European Cinema:

Before World War II, three major schools German Expressionism, Soviet Socialist & Italian Neorealism had contributed to the Cinema World. After 1960, Czeck, Polish, Hungarian films have also contributed a lot to the World Cinema.

Asian Cinema:

Apart from America and Europe, China, India, Japan, Iran, Korea, Taiwan and Hong Kong also come under the film making category of Asian Cinema. India produces the largest number of films in the world that too with its own unit.

African Cinema:

African films are mainly made raising issue of colonialism. Even Ousmane Sembene's "Black Girl" was the first film that won the international recognition as and he is regarded the "Father of African Cinema". Senegal is the most popular place of African Film Production. Egypt is another prominent filmmaking country of Africa. Majority of the Arabic language films have been made in Egypt. African countries like Morocco, Tunisia, Algeria are also making interesting films regularly.

Latin American Cinema:

After 1960, The latin American countries like Cuba, Argentina, Brazil, Mexico are also making films on social, historical, and political issues.

The History of Indian Cinema

The Wrestlers(1899) by H.S. Bhatavdekar showing a wrestling match at the Hanging Gardens in Mumbai was the first film ever to be shot by an Indian.

It was also the first Indian documentary film. In the Year 1913, Raja Harish Chandra, a silent film in Marathi, was the first full-length Indian motion picture, Produced-directed and written by Dadasaheb Phalke, who is called the Father of Indian Cinema.The female roles in the film were played by male actors. The film marked a historic benchmark in the film industry in India. Only one print of the film was made and shown at the Coronation Cinematograph on 3 May 1913. It was a commercial success and paved the way for more such films.

The **Dadasaheb Phalke Award** is the highest award in Indian cinema. It is presented annually at the National Film Awards ceremony by the Directorate of Film Festivals, an organisation set up by the Ministry of Information & Broadcasting, Govt. of India. The recipient is honored for their "outstanding contribution to the growth and development of Indian cinema" and is selected by a committee consisting of eminent personalities from the Indian film industry. Presently, the award comprises a Swarna Kamal (Golden Lotus) medallion, a shawl, and a cash prize of Rs. 1 lakh (Approx.1500 USD$)

Dadasaheb Phalke
(1971)
Pioneer of Indian
Cinema.

First presented in 1969, the award was introduced by the Indian Government to commemorate Dadasaheb Phalke's contribution to Indian cinema. Phalke (1870–1944), who is popularly known as and often regarded as "The Father of Indian cinema", was an Indian film-maker who directed

India's first full-length feature film, Raja Harishchandra (1913). Dhundiraj Govind Phalke, popularly known as Dadasaheb Phalke, was an Indian producer-director-screenwriter, known as the Father of Indian cinema. He was born on 30th April, 1870 in a Brahmin Marathi family at Tryambakeshwar, 30 km away from Nashik, Maharashtra, The Posts and Telegraphs Department is proud to celebrate the memory of this great sage of cinema by issuing a special commemorative stamp in his honour on 30th April, 1971.

The first recipient of the award was actress Devika Rani. So far, there have been 47 awardees. Among those, actor Prithviraj Kapoor is the sole posthumous recipient. His actor-filmmaker sons Raj Kapoor (1987) and Shashi Kapoor (2014), Lata Mangeshkar (1989) and Asha Bhosle (2000) along with Baldev Raj Chopra (1998) and Yash Chopra (2001) are the siblings who have won the award. The most recent recipient of the award is actor Manoj Kumar who was honoured at the 63rd in 2016 & Akshay Kumar won the best Actor in 64th National Film Award this year.

AVM Productions is an Indian film production studio. It is the oldest surviving studio in India. The filming studios are located in Vadapalani, Chennai, Tamil Nadu.

Question Bank 7

1. When Cinema came into existence?
2. Whodesigned the Camera for the 1st time in the world?
3. Who were the first filmmakers of the world?
4. What are the main era of Cinema?
5. Hollywood is famous for?
6. Who is called the father of Indian Cinema?

CHAPTER 2

The Television Era

John Logie Baird was a Scottish (UK) engineer, innovator, one of the inventors of the mechanical television, demonstrating the first working television system on 26 January 1926, and inventor of both the first publicly demonstrated colour television system, and the first purely electronic color television picture tube.

Television is not an art medium but a communication medium. By the late 1990's, maximum Americans had one TV set and spent 3-5 hours a day watching TV.

Commercial Transmission:

USA: The transmission of Television services began on 2nd July, 1928 in United States of America. The broadcasters were allowed to advertise for the first in 1941 in US. On 4th September, 1951, the first live national television broadcast in the U.S. was made when President Harry Truman's speech in San Francisco, California was transmitted. In 1964, color broadcasting began on Prime time television in USA.

Germany: It began in 1929 in Germany but it was without sound till 1934, even Berlin Olympic Games were transmitted in 1936.

UK: The first British television broadcast was made over the BBC radio transmitter in September, 1929. BBC followed a system of a television license fee on owners of television to generate revenue for decades and served BBC excellently.

Soviet Union (USSR): The Soviet Union began test broadcast in Moscow in 1931 and manufactured television sets in 1932 but Television programmes broadcasting began in 1938.

Video & Cable Networks:

Philips invented VHS-Video Home Service in 1970. It was tape recording instrument/machine that could be played through the player. It was followed by the inventions of VCD & DVD (Digital Versatile Dics). These were helpful in Non-broadcast situation. By 1960s, appeared the cable network that could offer an alternative to the major nation channels. They were called CATV (Community Antenna Television) system. The development of cable and satellite television in the 1970s allowed for more channels and encouraged businessmen to target programming towards specific audiences.

Satellite Communication: With the development of Satellite technology for communication, the scope for television transmission went up hugely in the 1980s.

Television coverage of the following events have attracted millions of viewers:

1. The US presidential election in 1960 wherein John F. Kennedy came into limelight as a charismatic leader.
2. Vietnam war in 1960s
3. Persian Gulf War 1991 covered by CNN
4. The assassination of Mrs. Indira Gandhi in 1984
5. IPL

Question Bank 8

1. Who invented Television?
2. When TV service began in USA?
3. What is the role of Satellite Communication?

CHAPTER 3

The Print Media

Journalism, a profession and even cultural industry and business, is three centuries old. It was made possible by a number of technologies as well as because of several social, political and economic developments.

Journalism in the 17th & 18th Centuries

By the 15th Century, letter press moveable type printing was widespread in the major centers of trade and learning all across Europe.

Letterpress is the oldest form of printing. In this method, a surface with raised letters is inked and pressed to the surface of the printing substrate to reproduce an image in reverse. Typically, metal type has been used but other possibilities include carved wood or stone blocks.

After the Gutenberg press introduced movable type to the process in the 15th century, letter press was the predominant printing method for 500 years. The creation of huge rotary presses made industrial printing and newspaper production practical.

During the reformation era the printing press came to be widely used by both Catholic and Protestant churches to propagate their beliefs.

Popularity of Print Media during Industrial Revolution

The Industrial Revolution played a very important role to make Print Media more popular. The telegraph facilitated the growth of news agencies such as Reuters, Associated Press, United Press International and Agence France Presse. By the 18th Century, news related publications in the United States of America and Britain managed to attract advertising support.

Press in India

India got its first newspaper called Bengal Gazette-weekly (also known as Hicky's Gazette or Calcutta Advertiser) in 1780, it carried advertisements right from the first issue.

Newspaper publishing is a big business today in India. The Times of India, The Indian Express, The Hindustan Times, The Hindu, Nav Bharat Times, Punjab Kesari, Dainik Jagran etc. are few popular National daily newspapers of India. According to RNI, the total number of registered publications, as on 31st March, 2015 are 1,05,443.

Feature of Journalism in the UK and USA

Newspaper are getting lesser in United States of America & Europe, unlike the huge growth of the print media in India, China and other Asian countries. According to the survey of World Association of Newspapers (WAN), based in Paris, the top ten newspapers of the world in terms of circulation are all Asian newspapers, the top three being from Japan. The major reason behind this is the remarkable growth of internet. Now, the news is easily available from online editions of newspapers, even from social networks and news blogs.

Online Edition of Newspapers

At the dawn of 21st Century, there was a high growth of Online Journalism. Almost every English and Indian language publication is easily available on World Wide Web. Indian websites that are at the forefront of online journalism are timesofindia.com, hindustantimes.com, indianexpress.com. The two Indian news agencies, Press Trust of India (PTI) and the United News of India (UNI) also have their own websites but they hardly publish all their news stories and features available for free.

News Alerts on Mobiles

Some Telecom services & news agencies provide 'news alerts' as a value addition service (VAS) on mobile phones, SMS messages for cricket scores, exam results, results of contests, emergency message etc. Now with the extensive use of internet, mobile apps have become more popular in the modern days. Social Media like Facebook, Linkedin, twitters, Whats app, etc. are getting more and more access Even AIR-Radio Station & Doordarshan-Television Channel have introduced news apps and with the help of them anybody can get the latest news update instantly on thair mobile itself.

The latest mobile (Smart /android) Phone has become the ultimate source to perform many functions. It's not only a device to talk to each other but it has many other features like camera, audio/video recorder, Messenger, watch, Planner, Forecast predictor, radio, torch, Social Media commander etc. Its really the Alladin ka Chirag.

UNIT-4

CHAPTER 1

The Combination of Media

All Media are the combinations of Natural human abilities and technologies developed/clubbed together. It can be majorly divided into 1. The art media & 2. The communication Media. The meaning of convergence in Media has two level 1. Artistic & 2. Technological.

The eminent Indian Historian V.K. Rajwade codifies the Evolutionary forms of Mass communication:

Natural ability	Functional use	Evocative use	Functional plus Evocative	External Means
Sound	Language	Singing	Verse	Instrumental music
Drawing	Alphabet	Painting	Illustrated Books	Photography
Gesture	Acting	Dance	Theatre	Puppetry
Solid Figure	Pottery	Sculpture	Architecture	Landscape, Town-planning

Convergence of Communication Media: (Nature of Media)

Print	It contains text
Radio	It's wireless communication that covers great distance instantly.
Cinema	Film is an analogous image captured in the camera, it can be seen in audio video format.
Television	It is an electronic image-its also in audio-visual format.

Today is the age of ICE-Information Communication Entertainment.

Undoubtedly, the Media and their capacity of creating and sharing information in many ways has important political and humanistic dimensions.

CHAPTER 2

Product & its Profile

Before launching any product in the market, a lot of things come under consideration-it's a long and on going process. Proper R & D (Research and Development) takes place like design, weight, color, look, packaging are the USP (Unique Selling Point) of any product. When the product is ready then advertising also play a very important role.

Specific Buyers-Every product belongs to a particular group of buyers which is set on the basis of their buying capacity and need. It can be mainly categorized as follows :

Computer

Electronic Gadgets

Mobile: Ordinary and Smart Phone

Vehicles-four wheelers & two wheelers

Beverage-Alcoholic & Non-Alcoholic

Entertainment

Financial

Snacks

Health Related

Home Appliances

ISP (Internet Service Providers) and search engine

Personal care

Travel Related

Retailers

How to Define Market: It depends upon many parameters:

1. Identify the customer need
2. Geographical dimension
3. Demographic-age, race, religion, gender, income, family size, occupation, education and marital status.
4. Behaviouristic
5. Psychographic

CHAPTER 3

Credibility of Advertising

It plays very a vital role to market any product. So, advertising is a very important tool that serves many purposes:

1. It introduces a new product in the market.
2. It helps to overcome its competitors.
3. It creates brand value through regular promotion
4. It crates sales & demand
5. It also promotes Visibility and on-going process to create trust and credibility among buyers.

Methods of Advertisements

Creative advt. Media campaign- through various forms like audio, still, visual, pamphlets, newspaper advertisement, billboard, advt. online, TV commercial, hoarding, boards, etc.

Whom to target-Local, national or International level. The prototypes are made as power point presentation. If it's a big campaign then it should be launched on TV, Radio, Print, Film. Billboards and internet etc.

Advertisement Through Exhibition with innovative ideas is also a good option to create market for a new product.

CHAPTER 4

How to Utilize in Media

After creating an advertisement, its very important to utilize the best available media to disseminate the message. The following are the best media available:

Print-Newspapers, Magazines, Brochures, Posters.

OOH-(Out of Home)-Billboards, Kiosks, Tradeshows, Events

Broadcast-Radio, TV, Digital, Mobile, Social Media

In film promos

Celebrity Endorsements

Games

Choice-The Best Media: It entirely depends upon the budget and targeted audience. If the target buyers are young then online is the best and for rural buyers then radio, newspapers, posters, television will be better choice.

Through eMail.

Top Indian News Agencies

The Prominent News Agency of India which provides the latest local, national, international: You may find out the important detail about all these news agencies:

Press Trust of India

Press Trust of India (PTI) is India's premier news agency, having a reach as vast as the Indian Railways. It employs more than journalists and stringers to cover almost every district and small town in India. Collectively, they put out more than 5,000 stories and 500 photographs a day to feed the expansive appetite of the diverse subscribers, who include the mainstream media, the specialised presses, research groups, companies, and government and non-governmental organisations.

PTI correspondents are also based in leading capitals and important business and administrative centres around the world. It also has exchange arrangements with several foreign news agencies to magnify its global news footprint.

Currently, PTI commands 90 per cent of new agency market share in India.

PTI was registered in 1947 and started functioning in 1949. Today, after 65 years of its service, PTI can well and truly take pride in the legacy of its work, and in its contribution towards the building of a free and fair Press in India. On its golden jubilee in 1999, President K R Narayanan said:"We got independence in August 1947.But independence in news and information we got only with the establishment of PTI in 1949.That is the significance of PTI..."

PTI Head Office New Delhi
The Press Trust of India Limited
PTI Building, 4, Parliament Street, New Delhi - 110 001.
Delhi area code 011.
EPABX: 23716621-24, 41394400, 41384460.
Fax: 23718714, 23715337 (Editorial) ,
23736882 (Economics), 23311694 (Bhasha)
email: gmadmin@pti.in http://www.pti.in/

The Press Trust of India Limited
357,Dr.Dadabhai Naroji Road,
UCO Bank Building,2nd Floor,
Fort Mumbai-400001.
Mumbai area code 022.
EPABX: 22872371 / 22872373 / 22872302
22873062 / 22871339.
Fax: 22870150, 22880816 (Editorial).
email: mumbai@pti.in

PTI Kolkata
The Press Trust of India Limited
7, Hare Street,
Kolkata-700001.
Kolkata area code 033.
EPABX: 22485261-64.
Fax: 22436187 (Editorial). email: kolkata@pti.in

PTI Chennai
The Press Trust of India Limited
1st Floor, No.10,First Main Road,
United Indai Colony,
Kodambakkam,
Chennai-600024.
Chennai area code 044.
EPABX: 23720226 / 23720231 / 23720241
23720235 / 23720221
Fax: 23720215. email: chennai@pti.in
011-41394495

About UNI The United News of India (UNI), founded in 1961, has emerged as one of the largest news agencies in India with several hundred subscribers across the length and breadth of the nation.

The agency's subscribers include newspapers published in 14 languages, All India Radio and Doordarshan, the Prime Minister's Office as well as Union Ministers' offices, Central and State governments, corporate and commercial houses besides electronic and web based media.

Having started its commercial operations on March 21, 1961, UNI has developed over the years to launch innovative steps and ideas that proved to be of immense benefit not only for its subscribers but to journalism as a whole. It has News Bureaus in all state capitals and other major cities. The agency also has representatives in key world capitals.

UNI was the first to start a multi-language news service UNIVARTA on May 1, 1982 that continues to provide Hindi newspapers and media organisations a comprehensive package of national, international, regional, sports and commercial news in their language of publication.

UNI pioneered a national news photo service in 1987. From despatching just about a dozen black and white photographs through courier to subscribers, it now uses the latest technology to make available digital colour photos numbering nearly 150 from all over the country. The agency also has a tie up with Reuters to supply international photos.

UNI remains the first and only news agency in the world to supply news in Urdu. UNI Urdu Service was launched by then Prime Minister PV Narasimha Rao on June 5, 1992. The service caters to newspapers, radio and television stations and government offices. Its ever expanding network covers Delhi, Uttar Pradesh, Madhya Pradesh, Bihar, Maharashtra, Karnataka, Andhra Pradesh and Jammu & Kashmir.

Contact us at :- United News of India
9, Rafi Marg, New Delhi-110001
Email:vsat@uniindia.com
Contact: 011-23714434 / 23357614 (O)
http://www.uniindia.com/

Indo-Asian News Service

The IANS Edge

- With India's growing importance in international strategic and economic thinking, news about the country is becoming more critical to the world. IANS provides news and analyses from India and South Asia from the region's perspective.
- IANS was established in 1986, initially to serve as an information bridge between India and its thriving Diaspora in North America.
- Three decades later, it is a full-fledged wire agency, putting out news 24x7 from India and South Asia, and covering events of interest to this region from around the world.
- IANS is, however, more than just India's largest independent news service. It is now the preferred source for all manner of content and information.
- A media powerhouse, IANS is divided into six business verticals: IANS News Service (English & Hindi), IANS Multimedia, IANS Publishing, IANS Media

Consultancy, IANS Software Services, IANS Mobile Services. Each vertical is headed by a distinguished professional with strong domain expertise.

- The IANS client list includes practically every major print publication in India, top television news channels, websites, mobile operators, ethnic publications abroad, central and state government ministries and departments, overseas Indian missions, corporates and public policy institutions.
- IANS is today one of India's most reliable, independent and professional news wholesalers, providing high quality content across all media platforms.

IANS India Pvt Ltd

A-45-50 Right Wing,
First Floor, Sector-16, Noida-201301 U.P.
+91-120-4822400
+91-9873188969 (Editorial) / +91-9654227330 (Reporting)
+91-120-4822403, +91-120-4822404
info@ians.in, support@ians.in, feedback@ians.in www.ians.in/

Asian News International

- Founded over 50 years ago, ANI is today South Asia 's leading multimedia news agency with over 100 bureaus in India , South Asia and across the globe. Our growth has been fuelled by the desire to fulfill the basic human need for knowledge and information, and we have done so with truth, credibility, quality and speed as our guiding principles.
- To cater to the ever-increasing spectrum of demand for news and information in an era of rapidly evolving technologies, our pursuit of excellence sees us ever innovating, improving and redesigning our products and services.

- As South Asia 's leading Multimedia News Agency, and one of the best professionally managed corporate media entities of the world, ANI has a big reputation to live up to. No wonder, we race with time every minute of the day and every day of the year, to deliver to our multitude of clients- television channels, radio stations, newspapers, websites and mobile carriers, both at home and abroad, the best possible video/audio, text and picture content.
- When it comes to covering South Asia , ANI goes across the globe to bring news of and from South Asia , wherever it takes place. The result is a complete service, multi-faceted in the depth of its coverage, and extensive in its reach.
- Today's digital era is seeing ANI fast emerging as a 'Complete Content House' providing text, video and picture content for TV, print, mobile and online media, all under one roof.
- For more information on any ANI Service:

Head Office:

ANI Building, Plot No. 15, Sector-9, R K Puram, New Delhi - 110 022

Email : rgaur@aniin.com

Tel : +91 9810057662

Landline : +91 11 26191058

Fax : +91 11 26191053email: ani@aniin.com or call us at our New Delhi News desk: 91-11-26189705, 91-11-26703000

http://www.aniin.com/

Samachar Bharti

- This is Indias's first bilingual news and photo wire service, dedicated to issues that are neglected by the mainstream media. It focus on national and global processes affecting the economic, social and political development of the people of India in particular and the region in general. It disseminate genuine as well as useful information to the nation and the people across the globe.
- Samachar Bharti Online News Agency (SBONA) is different from contemporary Indian news agencies in many ways. There has been a very strong feeling in the outside world that there is no credible and independent source of information in India, chiefly because the electronic media including radio and television networks are state-owned.
- Samachar Bharti is the first-ever Indian news agency operating English and Hindi news services simultaneously along with comprehensive national and international photo coverage. The news reports often appear in the national and international print media while The photographs dominate news pages in most of the newspapers coming out from New Delhi, Mumbai, Lucknow, Bhopal and Jaipur besides some leading papers in the Middle East, Europe and the United States.
- In English and Hindi languages, It offer information packages to suit diverse needs; both local and international publications, print and electronic media, dailies and weeklies, magazines and periodic journals, specialised and subject-specific publications. It is also

equipped for prompt dissemination of breaking news to the print and electronic media around the world.

- The constituent elements of Samachar Bharti are an independent policy, a pioneering spirit, a highly motivated professional core team, state-of-the-art technology, strategically located Bureaux and Correspondents spread all over India, and above all a sense of mission.

PIONEERING SPIRIT

- Samachar Bharti pioneered-and continues to be the only news agency to operate-photo service in India. Also, It is the only Indian media organisation that processes information in a substantially none-paper environment. The limitations remain correspondents, who must fax in, and to a lesser extent, processing of Hindi copy.

HIGHLY MOTIVATED PROFESSIONAL CORE TEAM

- Samachar Bharti core team is made up of some of the most distinguished figures of the industry in their respective spheres of skill, plus some of the most brilliant prospects. A delicate blend of experience and freshness, the crew, pitted against several practised combinations, has come out a winner in many situations.

STATE-OF-THE-ART TECHNOLOGY

- No media organisation in India is tapping computers and the Internet as extensively as Samachar Bharti. The desk is fully computerised, as is reporting and of course, dissemination. The photographers, too, are equipped with digital cameras.

- Power-packed PCs, most modern optical scanning devices, and fastest network and communications' cards have together contributed significantly to making Online a formidable opponent for the competition. In fact, although it is located south of the Digital Divide, we virtually operate north of it.

BUREAUX AND CORRESPONDENTS

- It is claimed that Samachar Bharti with its Central office in New Delhi and head office in Bhopal is a news network that has its bureaus at each provincial headquarters in India besides some major cities including Lucknow,Jaipur, Patna, and Ahmedabad. They are headed by senior, respectable and professional journalists. Their reporting teams comprise young, educated and honest reporters and photographers. It has sufficient correspondents represent Samachar Bharti in every district and tehsil headquarter of the country.
- This much for domestic network; as well, Samachar Bharti has its correspondents in important world capitals and major cities including Washington, New York, Koeln (Germany), Moscow, Tokyo, Chicago, London, Amsterdam, Dubai, Cairo, Saudi Arabia and Kuwait covering events round-the-clock.
- Working in tandem with core team, this extensive network of ears and eyes puts Online on top of the news ahead of the competition.

Contact

113, junior MIG, Old Subhash Nagar
Bhopal, India – 462023
Contact No.- 0755 424 5810
E-mail: samacharbharti24@gmail.com

Technical Director
1/3 Amber Complex, First Floor, Zone II,
M.P. Nagar, Bhopal, India – 462 011
Contact No.- 887102710
E-mail: dsrajawat@gmail.com
Bureau Head, Delhi
Contact No.- +91 94547 47190
E-mail: newdelhi@samacharbharti.in
Bureau Chief, Uttar Pradesh
Email: samacharbharti.up@gmail.com
http://www.samacharbharti.in/

Hindusthan Samachar

About Hindusthan Samachar

Presently the service is being provided in Hindi, Marathi, Gujrati, Nepali, Oriya, Asamiya, Kannad, Tamil, Malayalam, Telugu, Sindhi, Sanskrit, Punjabi and Bangla. Efforts are on to cover other languages too. The service is fully based on the web internet technology. The subscriber can either downloaded the next or convert it into E-mail format.

A number of regional language papers along with some of the leading Hindi Newspapers are the subscribers. Apart from this Some State Governments, Organization and Institutions are subscribing the news scan service.

Vital Role in Media

Hindusthan Samachar is doing a vital service to newspapers. While on the one hand it is providing news emanating from the state capital to small newspapers in rural areas in different languages, it is also providing news of rural areas and small segments to the national newspapers.

History

Beginning

- In order to give a vent to the voice of millions of indians, the Hindusthan Samachar was formed on 1st Dec. 1948.
- Formally in 1951 Bihar govt. subscribed to the Hindusthan Samachar followed by Uttar Pradesh, Maharashtra, Punjab, Haryana, Bihar, Rajasthan, Odisha, Assam, Karnataka and Kerala. From 1968, All India Radio also came on the subscriber's list. Nepal Radio also came on our subscriber's list since 1953. Subsequently Nepal T.V. also joined from 1964 onward Doordarshan also started using the news service.
- The achievement of the Hindusthan Samachar is a milestone in the development of the national media. Hindusthan samachar provided a new dimension to the regional papers. Through its news and analytical reports, it created awareness among the readers and it focused on social issues as well as developmental activities.

Facing of Challenges

- Emergency was clamped on 26th june 1975. There after all the news agencies were merged into a single unit called Samachar. After the restoration of democratic rights Hindusthan Samachar recommenced its functioning.
- But clouds loomed large on the horizon and due to some anavoidable reason Hindusthan Samachar stopped working in 1986.

A new Beginning

- The share holders of the Hindusthan Samachar thought it prudent to restart Hindusthan samachar news agency keeping in view call of the hour. In 2000 Hindusthan Samachar decided to restare with inovative measures to face the emerging challenges in the media sector so that it can acquire a place of prominence.
- Today Hindusthan Samachar provide news in 14 Indian languages. Effort are on to cover more.

Head Office

D – 160, Sector-63,
Noida – 201301, (NCR) Delhi
Ph :- 0120-4804480

Editor-in-Chief & CEO
Mob: 8130011615
Phone: 0120-4804480
Email: ceo@hindusthansamachar.com

Administration

General Manager (HR)
Mob: 8860185532
Phone: 0120-4804480
Email: gmhr@hindusthansamachar.com

General Manager (Administration & Welfare)
Mob: 9999971717
Phone: 01204804480
Email: gmadmin@hindusthansamachar.com

Chief Financial Officer
Mob: 7209959604/9818438794
Phone: 01204804480
Email: cfo@hindusthansamachar.com

Bureau Office Delhi

Address: M6, Bhagat singh Market,
Near Gole Market, Delhi-110001
Ph: 011-65439538, Fax: 011-43560629 Mail: hsdelhi55@gmail.com

Madhya Pradesh

Address : Plot No. 8, Zone-1,
Press Complex, M.P. Nagar, Bhopal
Mobile : 09425601264, fax - 0755-2761144
Email : hsnews24@gmail.com

Uttar Pardesh

1, Naveen Market, Kesar bagh,
Lucknow- 226001
Phone : 0522-2618910
Mobile : 09452875890
Email: hsup75@gmail.com

Jharkand

Address : 2nd Floor Nilamber Appartment,
Ashok Puram, Opp. Ashok Nagar Road No-04, Ranchi : 834001
Mobile : 09431597165
Phone : 0651-22440015
Email: hsranchi@gmail.com

Uttrakhand

Address: 48/52.old no. 32,
Keshav road opp. Arya samaj mandir,
laxman chowk, Dehradun- 248001
Mobile: 09410367071 Telefax: 0135- 2725451
Email: hsuttrakhand@gmail.com

Panjab & Haryana

Address: 736, Sector-12 A, Punchkula Haryana-134112
Mob.08353944290, 9455241497
Email: hs1chandigarh@gmail.com

Rajasthan

Address: D - 38, Jagan Path, Chomu House, Jaipur-302001
Mob : 9414047480
Email : hindusthansamacharjaipur@gmail.com, hsjpr1@gmail.com

Himachal Pradesh

Address: 2A, Baba Market, Shimla(HP)-171003
Email: hsshimla@gmail.com Mobile: 09418190914

Bihar

Address: H.O. Kapil Prasad, behid officer,
flat 30/60, friends colony, Hartali Chawk,
Bally Road, Patna: 800001
Mob: 08804919352
Email: hspatna@gmail.com, hspatna1@gmail.com

Chhattisgarh

Address: Bombay Bazaar, B-block, First Floor,
G.E. Road, Raipur-492001
Mob: 09425520515, 07711-4264411
Email : hs36garh@gmail.com

Jammu & Kashmir

Address : Room no. 13, Geeta Bhawan, Pared, jammu-181001
Mobile : 09419143528
Phone & Fax- 0191-265607
Email : balwan.hsjk@gmail.com, hsjk2009@gmail.com

Tripura

Dhaleswar, Nutan Palli Road No. 8 Agartala (W. Tripura)
Mob: 09436540930, 03812311332
Email : nabendubhattacharjeeagt@gmail.com

Arunachal Pradesh

Address: C/o Chuku Talo, B- sector QRT,No 35 ,
T-lll (near,Rajbhawan), Dist.Papum Pare-791111
Mob: 08794160796
Email: taguningee77@gmail.com

Andaman & Nicobar

Sharma Niwas, Mazar Pahad
Post-Shadipur, Portblair-744106
Mob: 09474240555
Email: rpsandaman@gmail.com

MEDIA UNIVERSITIES COLLEGES INSTITUTES IN INDIA.

Indian Institute of Mass Communication

JNU new campus,

Aruna Asif Ali Road,

New Delhi - 110067, India.

Phone: 267441062 ,26741073

Website: www.iimc.nic.in

AJK Mass Communication Research Centre

Jamia Millia Islamia University

Maulana Mohammed Ali Jauhar Marg

New Delhi -110 025

Phone: +91 11 2698 7285, +91 11 2698 6812,

+91 11 2698 6813

Email: mcrc@jmi.ac.in

Apeejay Institute of Mass Communication

Apeejay Campus, Institutional Area, Sector - 8, Dwarka, New Delhi - 110077

Mobile: 08447779011, 09818217281, 09868004678

Phone: 011-2536 7821

Telefax: 25367821 Fax : 25363985

E-mail: aimc.del@apj.edu

Dept. of Film & TV Studies

Bharatiya Vidya Bhavan

Kasturba Gandhi Marg,

New Delhi - 110001 (India)

Tel. : +91-11-23389449, 23388021
Mobile: 8744 005 005 8745 005 00
Website- www.film-tvstudies.com

Asian Academy of Film & Television

Marwah Studios,
FC-14/15, Film City, Sector-16A,
NOIDA, Uttar Pradesh
Toll Free: 1800-102-6066, Ph.0120-4831100
www.aaaft.com
Email ID: help@aaft.com

Massco Media

(MassCoMedia Job –Oriented Programs in association With Delhi University)
(A Unit of Delhi Press)
Campus of Open Learning
Mass Communication Courses
Journalism & Mass Communication, TV Journalism, Photography,
Production, Film Making, Advertising, PR & Event Management
Sector-58, NOIDA, Uttar Pradesh
M: 9650226111,9871446204,011-27181469
www.masscomedia.com

Shoots & Shoots Photography Academy

I-2, L.G.F., Jangpura ext.,

New Delhi-110014 (INDIA)

Tel:+91-11-41823641,

41515005, 8447885005, 9810615005

Email: shootsandshoots@gmail.com

R. K. Films & Media Academy

8A/8, W.E.A., Karol Bagh, (Behind MTNL Telephone Exchange on Pusa Road)

New Delhi - 110 005, India

Phone : (+91) 011-45064241

Mobile:(+91) 93122 31374 ,(+91) 93122 37583, (+91) 93100 47775

Email : info@rkfma.com

DQ School of Visual Arts

A-3, Rajouri Garden,

(Adjoining Raja Garden Fly Over)

Ph: 28160000

Mob: 09717695833

Email: rajouri@studiovista.in

South Ex-E18, 2nd Floor,SSouth Extension Part I,

New Delhi – 110049

Phone No: 011-24698301/02/03 Mob: 08860100025,24

Email: southex@studiovista.in

Preet Vihar-C-57, 1st Floor, Preet Vihar,
(Opp. Swasthya Vihar Bus Stop
& Metro Pillar 81)
Vikas Marg, New Delhi – 110092
Ph: 0011-430516006, 07, 08
Mob: 08860100026, 27
Email: preetvihar@studiovista.in

Pitampura-FD-8, 2nd Floor,
(near Madhuban Chowk, opp. Metro pillar no.368)
New Delhi 110034
Phone nos, 011-27314190, 91 & 92
Mobile: 08860100058 & 59
Email: pitampura@studiovista.in
DSYW DQ Animation Academy

Mudra institute of communications (MICA)

Shela, Ahmedabad - 380 058, Gujarat, India
Ph: +91 2717 308250, +91 2717 308349
Email: admissionenquiry@micamail.in
Website - www.mica.ac.in

Xavier Institute of Communications

5, Mahapalika Marg, St. Xavier's College, Mumbai - 400 001. INDIA
Ph: +91 22 2262 1366 / 2262 1639 Website-admin@xaviercomm.org

Sardar Patel College of Communication & Management

Bharatiya Vidya Bhavan

Kasturba Gandhi Marg, New Delhi - 110001

Tel. : + 91-11-23382005 / 23389942

Fax : + 91-11-23382003

E-mail: info@bvbdelhi.org

Manorma School of Communication

Erayilkadavu Kottayam - 686 001

Tel: 0481-2300851

Email: info@manoramajschool.com

Makhan Chaturvedi Rashtriya Patrakaeita Evam Sanchar Vishwavidyalaya

Campus address : B-38 Vikas Bhawan, Opp Dak Bhawan, Press Complex, Zone-1

M.P. Nagar, Bhopal - 462011

Old Postal address : P.O. Box No. RSN/560, Trilochan Singh Nagar, Shahpura, Bhopal-462016

Email: MCU.pravesh@gmail.com

Symbiosis Institute of Media & Communication

Symbiosis Knowledge Village,

Gram: Lavale, Taluka: Mulshi,

Pune - 412115 Maharashtra, India.

Ph. 02039116100, 08888864620

Website- www.simc.edu

Indian Institute of Journalism & New Media

Opp. BGS International Residential School

Nityanandanagar, Kumbalgudu

Kengeri Hobli

Bangalore 560 074; India

Telephone: 91-80-2545 2564 / 2545 2565; Fax: 91-80-25452563

Film and Television Institute of India

Law College Road, Pune - 411 004,

(Maharashtra) INDIA.

Tel : +91 - 020- 25431817 / 25433016 / 25430017

E-mail :Acedamic Office:academicofficeftiindiacom, academicsftii@gmail.com

Short Courses: shortcourse@ftiindia.com

Computer Section: multimedia@ftiindia.com

Satyajit Ray Film & Television Institute

E.M.Byepass Road, P.O. Panchasayar, Kolkata-700094

Phone-(033)2432 8355/8356/9300

Fax – (033)2432-0723/9436

Website- www.srfti.ac.in

National School of Drama

Bahawalpur House-1, Bhagwandas Road New Delhi – 110 001

Email: nationalschoolofdrama@gmail.com

Sri Aurobindo Society Campus

Shaheed Jeet Singh Marg, Adhichini, New Delhi -110017

E-mail: info@sac.ac.in

Whistling Woods International

Film City Complex, Goregaon (East), Mumbai-400065, Maharashtra, India.

Phone: +91-22-30916247 / 30916248

Email: admissions@whistlingwoods.net

Advertising Club Madras

57, Bazullah Road, T. Nagar, Chennai – 600 017

Ph: 044 28141581, 044 28142250, 044 42694778

Fax: 044 28142272

Email:info@adclubmadras.com, advertisingclubmadras@gmail.com

D.A.V College of Girls

Yamuna Nagar 135001

Ph 01732-224674 ,228152

Website- www.davyamunanagar.com

Jagran Institute of Management and Mass Communication

F-33, Sector-6, NOIDA, U.P. Pin -201301

Phone No. : 0120-2423950/51/52

E-mail : info.jimmc@gmail.com

Kushabhau Thakare Patrakarita Avam Jansanchar Vishwavidyalaya

Kathadih, Post Office : Sunder Nagar, Raipur
(Chhattisgarh) 492 013
e-mail : kulsachiv@ktujm.ac.in

Mahatma Jyoti Two Phoolo University

SP-2 & 3, Kant Kalwar RIICO Industrial Area,
NH-8 Near Achrol, Jaipur, Rajasthan, INDIA
Phone No.:-01426 - 283952, 283953

MREI Aravalli Campus

Sector – 43, Delhi – Surajkund Road,
Faridabad – 121004, (Haryana), India
Phone: +91-129-4259000 (30 Lines)
Fax:- +91-129-4198211, Email: info@mrei.ac.in

Mudra institute of communications

Shela, Ahmedabad - 380 058, Gujarat, India
Email-admissionenquiry@micamail.in
Ph-+91-2717-308313

Mumbai Educational Trust

Bhujbal Knowledge Centre
Bandra Reclamation, Bandra (West),
Mumbai - 400 050, Maharashtra, India
Board line: +91 22 2644 044

National institute of Event Management

Ground Floor, Nandanvan, Corner of Vallabh Bhai Road & Ansari Road,

Vile Parle Mumbai,Maharashtra 400 056.

Phone: 91 22 2671 6676, 91 22 2628 2928

Mail: support@niemindia.com

Sadhna Academy for Media Studies

C - 457, Sector 10, Noida - 201301, Uttar Pradesh

+91- 9999131400 +91- 9999131500

+91- 9999131800 0120-4039915

noida.sams@gmail.com

Sadhna TV, 38 Rani Jhansi Raod, Jhandewalan, New Delhi

+91- 9999131400 +91- 9999131500, +91- 9999131800

info@sadhnamedia.com

Scms Cochin School of Business

SCMS Campus, Prathap Nagar Muttom, Aluva Cochin – 683 106, Kerala, INDIA.

Ph: +91 484 2623803/4 Fax: +91 484 2623855

E.mail: scms@scmsgroup.org

Express Institute of Media Studies

The Indian Express Building 9&10, Bahadurshah Zafar Marg, New Delhi-110 002

Phone: +91-11-23465510

Fax: +91-11-23702141

Flame university

Gat No. 1270, Lavale, Off. Pune Bangalore Highway,
Vadzai, Dist. Pune - 412115, India

Guru Gobind Singh Indraprastha University

Sector - 16C Dwarka Delhi - 110078, India
Tel: +91-11-25302170, Fax: +91-11- 25302111

Guru Jambheshwar University of Science & Technology,

Hisar - 125001, Haryana (India)

Haridev Joshi University of Journalism and Mass Communication

Information Center, Sawai Ramsingh
Road, Jaipur-302004
Ph. No. +91-141-2373761, 2373739
Email Id. - info@hjuj.ac.in

University of Kashmir

Hazratbal, Srinagar, Jammu & Kashmir, India,190006
EMAIL: info@kashmiruniversity.net
ADMIN PHONE: +91 (194) 227 2096,
+91 (194) 227 2097

Kodaikanal Christian College

Kodaikanal Christian College,
Paradise Hill, Prakasapuram P.O.,
Kodaikanal, TN

Aligargh Muslim University

Aligarh 202002. (U.P)

Website- www.amu.ac.in

Amity University

Sec-125 Noida 201303(U.P)

Ph- 0120-2445252, Website- www.amity.edu

Annamalai University

Directorate of distance education

Annamalainagar 608002(T.N)

Website- www.annamalaiuniversity.ac.in

Ashok Inlead School of Hospitality

National expressway -8 81P sector-34 , gurgaon-122001

Toll free- 1800-1034-200, Website- www.inlead.In

City School of Social & Managerial Sciences

IInd floor , vijaya complex Anna nagar west , chennai 600101

Ph. 044-26153030, 26150303

Website- www.city-schools.com

Devi Ahilya Vishwavidyalaya

Ravindernath Tagore Margaret, Indore 452001(M.P)

Ph. 731-2527532

Website-www.dauniv.ac.in

Gujarat University

Navrangpura, ahemdabad 380009(GUJ)

Ph. 079-26301341

Website- www.gujaratunivetsity.org.in

Institute of Integrated Marketing Communication & Management

D-185 B&C , Okhla Phase I New Delhi 110020

Website- www.iimcm.net, Ph. 011-46646503

Madurai Kamraj University

Palkalainagar Madurai 625021(Tamilnadu)

Website- www.Mkudde.org

Met Institute of Mass Media

Bandra(west) Mumbai 400050

Toll free 1800220234

Website- www.met.edu

Nalanda Open University

2nd floor biscomaun bhavan Gandhi maidan , Patna 800001(Bihar)

Website- www.nalandaopenuniversity.com

Nmims University

V.L mehta road, vile parle Mumbai 400056

Website- www.nmims.edu

Sardar Patel College of Communication & Management

Bhartiya vista bhawan kasturba Gandhi marg , near India gate new Delhi 110001

Email- info@bvbdelhi.org

Sri Padmavati Mahila Vishwavidyalaya

Tiupati 517502 chittoor DIST.(A.P)

Ph. 0877-2248417

Website- www.padmavatiwomen-univ.org

Sharda University

Plot no. 32-34 , knowledge park III greater Noida 201306

Ph. 0120-3121001

Website : www.sharda.ac.in

Times Business School

A-39 , Kaliash Colony New Delhi 110048

Ph. 011-46574657

Website- www.times.ac.in

Kurukshetra University

Institute of Mass Communication & Media Technology

Website: www.kukinfo.com

University of Maysore

Crawford hall, Mysore 570005

Ph.0821-2419361

Website: www.uni-maysore.ac.in

Abbreviation & Media Terminology

A/V - Audio/Video

AAAJ - Advertising Agencies Association of Jamaica

AAEN - African American Entertainment Network

AAF - American Advertising Federation

AAIM - Asian American Independent Media

AAP - Australian Associated Press

ABA - Australian Broadcasting Authority

ABC - Associated British Cinemas

ABC - Audit Bureau of Circulations

ACMC - Asian Congress for Media and Communication

ACP - Associated Collegiate Press

ACTF - Australian Children's Television Foundation

ABC - Australian Broadcasting Corporation

AMPAS - Academy of Motion Picture Arts and Sciences

AP - Associated Press is the essential global news network, delivering fast, unbiased news from every corner of the world to all media platforms and formats.

BBC - British Broadcasting Corporation

PTV - Pakistan Television

LSTV - Lok Sabha Television

RSTV - Rajya Sabha Television

DD-Delhi Doordarshan

Accreditation: Accreditation for those working in the media means that an association, like a government agency, military organization or corporation has verified that a reporter works for a recognized publication or media outlet. Often referred to as a press pass, it makes the journalist eligible for special access rights and treatment.

Agenda Setting

The theory behind agenda-setting suggests that the media determines what issues the public should think about and when they should think about them.

Audience

The audience makes up the readers, listeners, and viewers of the news. Without the audience, there would be absolutely no market for journalism, as they are the reason journalists write.

Audience Research

Audience research measures the viewership, readership, listenership, and web traffic for media publications. This not only assists the companies in finding out how large their audience is, but it also helps advertisers see who the audience is also.

Advertorial -An advertisement in the form of an editorial is called an advertorial.

Anchoring

Anchoring is the practice of presenting the news on television, the radio, or the Internet. An anchor is the person who actually delivers that news to the audience. This usually takes place from a studio, with an entire crew assisting with the production. The news that is delivered is either stories written by reporters or provided by wire services and rewritten.

Audit Bureau of Circulations (ABC) - Independent, non-profit organization comprised of publishers, advertisers, advertising agencies to audit and certify circulation of various publications. Audit reports show the average net-paid-circulation of the publications (including daily and weekly editions of newspapers, and magazines) and is used by advertisers in planning their marketing campaigns.

Background report

Journalists utilize a wide variety of means when gathering information on their subjects. One of the ways to find information such as criminal, financial, and commercial histories is through a background report.

Blog

Blogs, online sites that allow discussions or consecutive informational posts, are relatively newer tools to the journalism. They allow writers, or in the blogging world "bloggers", to regularly and freely post their thoughts, ideas, and research in an open environment.

Broadcast

One of the main ways the news is distributed is through broadcasting. Broadcast is either live or pre-taped television or radio circulation. Its main focus is the ability to get the message to the listeners or viewers in the most efficient and effective way possible.

Byline: The byline on a newspaper or magazine article gives the date, as well as the name of the writer of the article.

B-roll

B-roll footage helps enhance and enrich the news story being told. It includes additional footage, animations, graphic design, or photographs, all pertaining to the story at hand.

Bleed - Printing that extends to the trimmed edge of a printed page.

Broadsheet - A full-size newspaper, measuring roughly 14 by 23 inches.

Cameraman

Those who operate the cameras in order to help relay news stories and information are cameramen.

Caption

Caption specify the details of photos. Photo captions help readers understand the meaning behind a particular picture, illustration, or photo that is either inside an article or alone on a page.

Caricature

Caricature is a drawing that makes someone look funny or foolish because some part of the person's appearance is exaggerated. : someone or something that is very exaggerated in a funny or foolish way.

Cartoonist

A cartoonist is the comedic artist of the journalism world, creating drawings that represent current events and relevant life circumstances.

Censorship

The legal definition of media censorship is the proscribing of speech, broadcast or writing held to be indecent, controversial or obscene. This is forbidden under the First Amendment of the Constitution in the United States, which specifically protects freedom of speech and freedom of the press. Though against the law, informally it still happens.

Citation

Citation in reporting is more accurately called attribution. It means the citing of sources by a journalist in his story. It is a key component of journalism ethics and gives credibility to a story by backing it up with documentation and references.

Clipping Service

A clipping service is most commonly known as a media monitoring service or a press clipping service. It supplies consumers with different documentation and forms of media content established from their interests. Clipping services are usually used to obtain content such as print, editorials, and sometimes advertising.

Column/Columnist

Journalists occasionally write regular pieces for publications. These are considered columns and the journalists that write them are columnists.

Comics

Comics are known to take up a special section of newspapers, being an audience favorite for generations. They consist of illustrations, text, and a short story, otherwise called a comic strip.

Commentary

Commentary is the discussion or explanation of events or situations that contributes to the audience's understanding of what is happening as well as the writer's point of view. The most common type of commentary in journalism would be in sports, where a commentator will give a live play-by-play on the happenings of the sports event.

Commentator

Commentators are mostly on the field, providing live action commentary on certain events, conducting interviews, and replaying feats. The most common type of commentator is under the sports umbrella, as well as political.

Community Manager

When a publication needs someone to be the face of their company, they look for a Community Manager. Based more in the digital world, they are in control of handling the social media, event planning, public relations, and communications. Community Managers control online content like blogs and newsletter, as well the social media pages like Facebook and Twitter.

Copy Editor

Copy editors review written works and make sure they are free from any errors or issues. They examine for spelling errors, structural issues, and punctuation mistakes, as well as inspect for accurate facts and data.

Content Manager

A content manager runs website content and organizes reports.

Copyright

Copyright means that the creator of a work, in this case usually written, visual or spoken, has exclusive rights to its use, distribution in order to profit from it. Journalists rely on the fair use doctrine to let them use any type of work that is copyrighted in limited circumstances without obtaining permission of the owner or paying for its use.

Corporate publishing

Corporate publishing is a corporation's own media and communications under their own umbrella. Any information that aids the work with editorial or journalistic work and is not run independently is considered corporate publishing. Whether print, broadcast, or online, this form of publishing helps companies market their brand and sponsor their image.

Corporative Television

Corporative television is broadcasting media throughout a corporate organization or company. With corporate funding, the broadcasting possibilities are vastly more open than independent publications. Today, corporate television runs both on television itself and through streaming internet.

Critics

Critics are journalists who professionally give their opinion and criticize products, articles, books, music, and much more. They portray a quality analysis of everything around, allowing readers or viewers to get a clear look before deciding on either purchasing or pursuing that said venture.

Center spread - An advertisement appearing on two facing pages of a newspaper, printed on a single sheet in the center of a publication.

Circulation - The total average number of distributed copies of a publication during a specified standard time (day, week or month).

Classified advertising - Advertising arranged according to categories featuring items offered for sale at a set price for a set period of time. Ad is generally in small print.

Classified display advertising - Classified advertising with the characteristics of display advertising – larger-sized, non-classified fonts, graphics and borders.

CMYK - An acronym for cyan, magenta, yellow and black - the four ink colors used in full color printing

Column inch - Publication space that is one column wide by one-inch high, used as a measure of advertising space. Column inches are used to determine the cost of ads.

Coverage Area - The geography of where a media has coverage. In print, the coverage area equates to the circulation area.

Display Advertising - Print advertisement that is placed outside of classified advertising. Display ads can range from small to the full size of the print page. Ads generally contain typeset copy, graphics and design to attract customer interest. The size of the ad is based on number of columns wide by number of inches tall.

Desktop publishing

It allows for the development and formation of layouts using a computer. With the turn of the century, journalists and news publications have come to use desktop publishing more often than not due to the flexibility and technology it provides.

Distribution

The term distribution refers to the way the publications deliver the product to their clients. News distribution takes places is numerous ways, from print to online.

Direct Quote

When a journalist quotes a source using their exact words, it is considered a direct quote.

Documentary

Documentaries are films that are primarily nonfiction, focusing on education and facts. A large portion of documentaries concentrate on the enlightening society on the events or important people in the world. They can be dramatized and often portray a particular thought or message in which the filmmakers believe are important to be told.

Editing

Editing is the action of verifying and correcting the information in a publication or broadcast before it is released to the public.

Editorial

Editorials are written by the senior staff or publishers of publications, often containing the personalized opinions of the publication itself.

Dots per inch (dpi) - The number of electronic dots per inch that a printer can print effecting resolution. The higher the dpi, the higher the resolution.

Free circulation - A publication sent to customers without their need to pay for it.

Frequency discount - A discounted advertising rate that is given by media to advertisers for placing multiple ad placements within a given time frame.

Feature

An article focusing on specific people or events is called a feature. Features are incredibly popular in the journalism world as they help the writer focus on thoughts, notions, and objections on various subjects and topics.

Foreign correspondents

Foreign correspondents are exactly that: correspondents stationed in foreign countries. They are needed for any breaking news stories or important information from the country they are in, or are sometimes required to travel. They cover anything from politics to wartime activities, or even the living conditions around them.

Freelance Journalist

Unlike journalists on payroll, freelance journalists cover a wide range of topics without being tied down to one set publication. They can choose to specialize in a single topic or cover just about everything. They suggest their own story ideas to the editors and if they get approved, they go about writing them for submission. Since they are freelancers, they can work for more than one publication at a time, opening up numerous options.

Freedom of Information Act (USA)

The Freedom of Information Act, or FOIA, became law in the United States in 1966. Its goal is the disclosure of government documents and information to the public. The law specifies which government agency records need to be disclosed, the procedures for the disclosure and nine exemptions. The federal law was updated by the Sunshine Act in 1976 as well as several other changes over the following decades. Many states also have Freedom of Information Acts.

Gutter - The blank space between margins of facing pages of a publication or the blank space between columns of text.

Hard news

News that covers politics, crime, war, disasters, and current events are all considered topics that fall under the umbrella of hard news.

Hoax

A hoax is a story that is intentionally written with false information but passed to be the truth. Hoaxes can include various rumors or urban legends. If a journalist deliberately published a story that was untruthful under the guise of being the truth is not only a hoax, but unethical when done outside of a joking manner.

Imprint

Print books are published under a trade name, which is called the imprint.

Internship

A wide variety of publications put together internships in order to help young journalists train and get a feel for working with a professional company. Internships allow for specialized on-the-job training and experiences for those who aspire to be journalists.

Illustration

Illustrations are forms of drawings, sketches, photographs, or graphic designs depicting what the author or artist is trying to portray in their piece.

Insert - A one-page or multi-page print advertisement that is distributed and inserted into a publication.

Island Ad/Position - A print advertisement surrounded entirely by editorial and not other ads.

Junior Art Director - In the advertising industry, a

junior art director is responsible for creating visual concepts in response to clients' briefs and relaying them to the art director.

Key Number - A code placed in an advertisement to facilitate tracking data.

Lead

The main introduction or beginning configuration of an article is called a lead. A lyricist or lyrist is a person who writes lyrics-words for songs-as opposed to a composer, who writes the song's melody.

LCD : An acronym for "Liquid Crystal Display". A text/graphics display technology where minute electrical currents change selected parts of the display screen.

Media bias

The prejudice and partiality of the media when it comes to the events that are both covered and told is considered media bias. There are countless international organizations that help look over and protect against media bias, as it is considered to be against the social and ethical guidelines of journalists.

Media law

Media law covers a wide range of topics, encompassing over all sub-categories of the mass media. With the increase of media popularity throughout the years, the need for media law has become a new and growing demand. It is a field in which those looking to enter the media business venture into, hoping to gain the knowledge and expertise they need in the field. Whether they are studying broadcasting or censorship, it all falls under the category of media law.

Media policy

It highlights the various guidelines and strategies expected of the corporation in regards to media relations. Establishing clear and concise media policies is imperative as it helps every employee, journalist, and manager understand what all is expected of them when it comes to handling other media outlets. Media policies exist outside of news corporations, present in businesses all over in order to ensure privacy as well as professionalism.

Magazine Supplement - A separately printed magazine section inserted into a newspaper. Supplements can be produced both locally and nationally.

MHZ : An abbreviation for "Megahertz". A measurement of frequency equivalent to one-million hertz.

NAB : "National Association of Broadcasters". An association which has standardized the equalization used in recording and reproducing. NAB lobbies for the interests of broadcasting as a delivery mechanism.

News Syndication

The action of distribution news content, including articles and columns, to various publications is known as print syndication.

News desk

A news desk handles the assigning of tasks to journalists and staff, controlling the coordination of stories and operations at publications. The news desk department directly influences the collection and reporting of the news as well, ensuring journalists receive assignments on a timely matter. They prepare the news reports and can regulate what is or is not released to the public

Newspaper Preservation Act (USA)

The Newspaper Preservation Act of 1970 in the U.S. allowed competing newspapers to set up joint operating agreements in the same market area, making them exempt from parts of the anti-trust laws. The goal was to keep competing newspapers publishing in areas where readership was declining.

Net Paid Circulation - A term used by ABC for the circulation of a publication to indicate the number of copies sold per issue both in subscription and newsstands.

Production-Pre-production is the process of fixing some of the elements involved in a film, play, or other performance. There are three parts in a production: pre-production, production, and post-production. Pre-production ends when the planning ends and the content starts being produced.

Post House : Abbreviation for Post production House. Mostly a company specialized in the business of cutting, color grading, finishing or conforming a clip, movie or film.

Post Production: All production work performed after the raw video footage and audio elements have been captured. Editing, titles, special effects insertion image enhancement and audio mixing are done during post production.

PCR - The production control room or studio control room (SCR) is the place in a Television Studio in which the composition of the outgoing program takes place. An SCR is also often the acronym for the Satellite Control Room, from here TV feeds are sent to & received from the local Satellite used by the TV station.

Periodical

A regularly published newspaper or magazine can also be considered a periodical. They can be released on a weekly, biweekly, or even monthly schedule and still be considered a periodical, as long as it is in regular intervals. Newspapers and magazines are not the only examples of periodicals. This term also encompasses academic journals, yearbooks, newsletters, novels that are released in intervals, or literary magazines.

Photo Journalist

A photo journalist is a journalist that tells their story using their photography. Usually on the front lines of whatever event happening, they get great images that stick to the news. Some photo journalists use video instead of photographs, still sticking to telling their side of things visually. They cover relevant events ranging from sports to international affairs. Publications hire their own photo journalists and some work freelance on their own.

Producers - help write the scripts for anchors, gather leads for stories, and put together live shots for the production. They keep a steady communication going between the anchors, directions, and the crew during filming, as well as making sure the broadcast ends on time. They also keep in contact with the reporters or correspondents to monitor the progress of their stories.

Proof-Reader

A proofreader has a very similar job to a copy editor, where they verify material for any grammatical, spelling, or layout errors before the piece goes further in the process. They are in constant contact with the writers, working between them and the publishers to ensure the best articles are produced.

Paid circulation - The number of printed copies that are purchased by readers in a given time period.

Pass-along readership - Readers of a publication in addition to the initial buyer. Also called Secondary Audience.

Preprint - Advertising inserts that are printed in advance of the regular press run and then combined with the final publication just prior to distribution.

Publisher's Statement - A notarized statement from the publisher of total circulation, geographic distribution, method of getting subscriptions, etc.

R&D : An acronym for "Research and Development".

RF : An acronym for "Radio Frequency". A term used to describe the radio signal band of the electromagnetic spectrum i.e. 3 MHz — 300 GHz. RF connectors carry RF television signals.

Radio Jockey - RJ is a person who hosts a talk show on radio.

Readership - The percent or number of persons who read a publication or advertisement.

Readers Per Copy - Number of readers per one copy of a newspaper or magazine.

Regional Edition - A national publication's geographic-specific section that provides circulation in a certain geographic area.

ROP Color - Color printing that is done during the scheduled press run and is placed in the regular space of the publication.

Run of paper or RUN oF paper (ROP) - Newspaper advertising that is positioned to run anywhere in a publication, with no exact choice of a specific c position or page. Placement is at the discretion of the newspaper.

Satirist

A satirist is a cartoonist or comedian that incorporates tough irony or sarcasm to bring to light social issues and criticism. The idea behind their work is not actually to make the audience laugh, but to make them consider the topics going on around them.

Soft News

Soft media is news and information we receive from media forms like television, articles, and magazines that mostly handle material including entertainment and lifestyle.

Sound Engineer

In charge of recording sounds and directing the audio effects, sound engineers work in all different fields. They need to be able to fix their equipment and be able to ensure it is always up and running, ready for production.

Stringer

Stringers are freelance journalists who are paid for each piece of their work individually by a publication. They do not receive a regular salary or benefits, but they do establish relationships with either one or more publications by showcasing their work and providing quality content when needed. Stringers can either be reporters or photographers, usually relied on when staff journalists are unable to reach newsworthy content in a timely matter.

A screenplay writer, screenwriter for short, scriptwriter or scenarist is a writer who practices the craft of screenwriting, writing screenplays on which mass media such as films, television programs, comics or video games are based.

Spot colour - An single extra color ink added to a page.

Supplement - A newspaper section in magazine format inserted prior to distribution.

Spot Boy does all the odd jobs starting from throwing light on the set to bringing tea for the crew.

Casting Director - The "CD" remains as a liaison between director, actors and their agents/managers and the studio/network to get the characters in the script.

Thumbnail : A down-converted image to provide a preview of its original material. Thumbnails are used to show the contents of video clips in still images.

TIFF : An acronym for "Tag Image File Format". It is the standard file format for high-resolution bit-mapped graphics. TIFF files may be compressed or uncompressed.

T.R.P.

Television Rating Point is a tool provided to judge which programmers are viewed the most. This gives us an index of the choice of the people and also the popularity of a particular channel.

Tabloidization

Tabloidization is when a newspaper is altered into a tabloid format. Most news publications focus on affairs such as politics and what is termed as hard news. When this is transformed into mostly celebrity gossip and entertainment news, it resembles more of a tabloid publication. This can either hurt or improve the ratings of a publication, depending on the audience and the nature of the content that was originally published.

Tabloid - A newspaper format that's roughly half the size of a broadsheet newspaper. Approximate size of a standard newspaper folded in half.

Tear Sheet - A publication page with an advertiser's message, sent to the advertiser as proof of accurate placement.

Videocast

A videocast is a video broadcast, usually live on the Internet. Often considered a video podcast, several news publications or journalists release videocasts as an updated feed. Some businesses find this method to be a great form of advertisement as it is low cost and easily shared.

Video Jockey - is an announcer who introduces videos on commercial music television station. VJ introduces music videos on TV, host entertainment programs, discuss/ review videos, and promote/interview artists.

Vlog

A video blog, most commonly referred to as a vlog, is a way that journalists can actively cover interests and topics via video entries in a blog format. Vlogs usually join together all of the aspects of a standard blog, but with a regular video stream. A regular host for vlogs is YouTube, which is a free platform that journalists can post their videos. They can also post their YouTube videos to social media, websites, or their other blogs if they wish.

Voice-Over - is a production technique where a voice- that is not part of the narrative (non-dietetic)—is used in a radio, television production, filmmaking, theatre, or other presentations. The voice-over is read from a script and may be spoken by someone who appears elsewhere in the production or by a specialist voice talent. It is usually pre-recorded and placed over the top of a film or video and commonly used in documentaries or news reports to explain information. Voiceover is used in video games and on-hold messages, as well as for announcements and information at events and tourist destinations. It may also be read live for events such as award presentations.

Wire services - help provide newsworthy information to publications everywhere. Much like news agencies, wire services gather information and sell the reports to whatever news organizations are subscribing to their services. Other than news, they can also provide stock photos, stock market information, and more. Wire services assist news publications immensely, allowing them to receive updated news quickly, efficiently, and accurately.

(**Source :** www.mediascope.com.au & www.openschoolofjournalism.com)

My Quotes

1. “The patriot, dedicated leader, Teacher, Scholar, Artist, Filmmaker, Sportsperson & Journalist are very important pillars of any nation or civilization. Because the past, present and future of any country moves on the axis of them only, their contribution remain the asset forever for the whole society.”
2. Wherever you move, there is news, It’s up to you, how you views.
3. Radio is the Pulse of the People around the World & to know the World around us even at the root level.
4. You should always explore what you are passionate for so that you can give your 100% to it & achieve what you are born for..
5. Creativity makes you more energetic.
6. You cannot restrict or control nature it develops & flourishes of its own, so, empower each other instead of exploring each other!!!
7. Life is a Journey let’s make it memorable with everyone whosoever come across in our life.

8. Your time, energy, wisdom are the biggest investment, try to invest them properly, respectfully in healthy environment. The dividend will come to you automatically with highest contentment.
9. You can't carry your position, degrees/medals all the times with you. But Its your wisdom, work, behavior that carry you everywhere!!!.
10. Empowering female means empowering the society.
11. The well wishers remains with you always, its not a matter whether they are physically or morally with you.
12. Never forget the sweet memories of the past years, But explore some more milestones waiting for you ahead.
13. A visionary media person can make a bright future of any nation.
14. Your work is your recognition that's your real reward.
15. Humanity is bigger than any religion or citizenship.
16. Every day starts with enormous opportunities, but it matters how & when we can utilize & convert them in to successful story.
17. Visionary & Passionate person can create history daily with his/her sincere virtue.
18. Media, without Image, is like a body without soul.
19. You can achieve whatever you like or desire to achieve But it needs your extra efforts and keen involvement.
20. The Sun is an inspiration. Rain, Thunder & Clouds are momentary, they cannot stop it to shine.

MEDIA QUIZ

1. Who is the founder of Facebook?
2. What is the name first Indian newspaper?
3. Under which Ministry R.N.I. works?
4. Who is the founder of Film City, Noida?
5. In which year Television programme started in India?
6. What is the full form of P.C.I.?
7. Amin Shyani is associated with which media?
8. Where is Satyajit Ray Film & Television Institute situated?
9. Sunder Pachai is the CEO of which Company?
10. Name the author of the book Titled: "Discovery of India"
11. Who is known as the Father of Indian Cinema?
12. Name the first Soap Opera (Family TV serial) on Indian Television.
13. Which is the first Indian TV Channel?
14. Which is called the first Print Media book?
15. Who received the prestigious 1st Kuldeep Nayyar Journalism Award-2017?
16. What is the full form of AIR?
17. Which country produced the Print paper first time in the world?

18. Famous Journalist Rajdeep Sardesai is associated with which Media Group?
19. Late TV Journalist Surender Pratap Singh was associated with which TV Channel?
20. Who is the present Chairman of Press Council of India?
21. What is the full form of ISBN?
22. Which Indian won the noble prize who is fighting against Child labour?
23. When I.T. Act introduced in India?
24. When Copy Right Act introduced in India?
25. What is the full form of INS?

Answer

1. Mark Elliot Zuckerberg, **2**. Bengal Gadget,

3. Information & Broadcasting Ministry,GOI,

4. Mr.Sandeep Marwah, **5**. In 1965, **6**. Press Council of India,

7. Radio, **8**. Kolkata, **9**. Google, **10**. Pt .J. L. Nehru,

11. Dada Saheb Phalke, **12**. Hum Log, **13**. Doordarshan,

14. The Bible, **15**. Mr.Ravish Kumar, **16**. All India Radio,

17. China, **18**. India Today Group **19**. Aaj Tak,

20. Justice Chandramauli Kumar Prasad

21. International Standard Book Number, **22**. Kailash Satyarthi,

23. In 2000, **24**. In 1957 **25**. Indian Newspapers Society.

Media Days Celebration

DAY	DATE
Wikipedia Day	15 January
Facebook launched Day	4th February
International Journalism Day	12th February
Radio Day	13 February
YouTube Foundation Day	14 February
World Press Freedom Day	3rd May
World Sports Journalists Day	2 June
World Photography Day	19th August
International Internet Day	29th of October
National Journalism Day	17th November
World Television Day	21 November

REMARKS ABOUT BOOK & AUTHOR

The relationship between media and students is not new, however, over generations it has taken many turns. Now, it is important to explore this relationship afresh. Hope that the book 'Media Can do wonders' in Students' Life' by S.S. Dogra will be an important contribution in this direction.

Gauhar Raza Ex.Prof. ACSIR, Chief Scientist & Filmmaker

+++

"मीडिया विद्यार्थी जीवन में चमत्कारिक साबित हो सकता है" विषय पर एस. एस. डोगरा जी द्वारा लिखित पुस्तक सच में मील का पत्थर साबित होगी. क्योंकि आज के माहौल में मीडिया जैसे अहम् विषय के प्रति युवा पीढ़ी में सकारत्मक सोच एवं दिलचस्पी पैदा करना बेहद ज़रुरी है।

अनुराग दीक्षित-एंकर-लोकसभा टी.वी.

+++

Mr. S.S. Dogra is self motivated media teacher and science communicator. He is working at grass root level to communicate Media among masses and students. I hope his latest book will help students to take maximum benefit from media resources for their life and career.

Nimish Kapoor (Scientist 'E' & Head, Science Films' Division, VIGYAN PRASAR Govt. of India, Noida, INDIA

This book is indispensible for any resource who is interested in "Media" for professional career. A great volume by Author -Shri S.S. Dogra ji for future generation .Media is one of the strongest tool of expression in today's neo world. It largely affects our Psyche & the entire thought process. Hence, the book "Media can do wonders' in Students' Life" is a must read for one & all.

Pallavi Prakash-Author, Corporate Trainer & Filmmaker

+++

आज "मीडिया" हर किसी की जिंदगी का एक अहम् हिस्सा बन चुका है वैसे ही विद्यार्थी भी अब धीरे-धीरे मीडिया को अपना पसंदीदा विषय बना रहे है. मेरा तो मानना है कि "मीडिया" विषय को अनिवार्य विषय बना देना चाहिए ताकि हर बच्चा इसका भरपूर लाभ उठाकर अपना उज्जवल भविष्य बना सकें। **मनीष आजाद-रेडियो जॉकी, एफ एम रेनबो, आल इंडिया रेडियो**

+++

"Media influences the life of students and their learning preferences and habits. It is the responsibility of all those concerned to help pupil to use media wisely so that learning become an enjoyable one. The book by S.S. Dogra is a highly useful handbook not only for the students but also for media practitioners, teachers and parents."

Dr. K. Y. Benedict-Principal, Mar Theophilus Training College, Trivananthapuram, Kerala

+++

For the students one of the important sources of information is the media. For them the written word constitutes the truth. The media must realize there significance in this regard and should not let them down by maintaining authenticity, credibility and the like. S.S. Dogra has endeavored to live up to this expectations honorably. My best wishes to him! ***Satish Sharma-Editor & Publisher, Garhwal Post,-the Prrmier English Daily of UK.***

+++

Eyes can convey understanding or annoyance, empathy or arrogance, approval or disapproval, encouragement or dis encouragement. Similarly, role of Media has been very helpful in 2017. It not only broadcast or print news of the regions and universe but it also educates students of all ages. Print, electronic and social are the platforms of Media reporting. Long Live Media! The contribution of S.S. Dogra in the field of media is splendid. I can say him a real media man. ***Netrapal Sharma-Senior Journalist-P.T.I.***

+++

कहते हैं कि परखी निगाह और दूर दृष्टि हमेशा एक नई सृजन को जन्म देती है. एस. एस. डोगरा जी की मीडिया के बारे में अनुभवी सोच और आने वाली पीढ़ी के लिए उनका समर्पण भाव इस पुस्तक में दिखता है. यह किताब न केवल एक दस्तावेज है बल्कि सहेज कर रखने लायक एक विरासत है. मेरी शुभकामनाएँ इस पुस्तक और इसके गहन एवं प्रभावशाली लेखक एस. एस. डोगरा जी के साथ हैं।

हरविंदर मंक्कर-फिल्म लेखक एवं निदेशक

+++

I congratulate Mr. S.S. Dogra for bringing out the book, 'Media can do wonders in Students' Life'. It is an important issue, hitherto mostly ignored. We are living in a world immersed in media. It reaches us from all possible directions, day in and day out. It shapes our thinking, perception and lives. Mr. Dogra has done a commendable job in showing the path to the students of making use of this mine of jewels, i.e. the media can be used not only for developing a general awareness of the world around us, but also in teaching and research. With good wishes to Mr. S.S. Dogra and the readers. ***Prof. (Dr.) Prasannanshu-Professor, National Law University, Delhi.***

+++

It is a great pleasure to me that Mr. S.S. Dogra ji publishing his first book on Media. I have been with him since last 12 years and witnessed his struggle in life, passion for work, versatility and his eagerness to take up multiple works to finish in 24x7 way attitudes. "Media can do Wonders and shape a better society if tackled in a positive way. As students are unbiased and can be shaped positively, so that they can utilize Media tool for making a better society. I wish all the best for his book "Media Can do Wonders' in Students Life" and pray for him to achieve all his dreams. ***Sanjay Mishra-IT Head, Dwarka Parichay***

+++

आपकी किताब ''मीडिया कैन डू वंडर्स इन स्टूडेंट्स लाइफ'' उम्मीद करता हूं कि देश की भावी पीढ़ी के भविष्य को नयी दिशा देने के लिये लाभकारी साबित होगी. डोगरा जी को ढेर सारी शुभकामनाएँ.

राजेश राय-खेल संपादक यूनीवार्ता (समाचार एजेंसी)

digg
flickr
You Tube
flickr